CONTENTS

FOREWARD

I've always been fascinated by myths and legends. In a world of facts and figures, it's a frequently startling glimpse into how people *felt* about things in the past. Oh, so often muddied by modern interpretation, or altered over hundreds – or in some cases – thousands of years of re-telling, cultural shifts, and changing priorities... but nevertheless a little bit of insight into those ancient times that we might otherwise not experience.

It's easy to discount these tales as fairy-stories that we should leave behind when we stop being children, but this would be a mistake. That connection to our past, however tenuous, is important. It helps to bridge the gap between people, then and now, and gives life to those who might otherwise be relegated to becoming dry facts on a dusty page in a desiccated tome on a researcher's shelf.

The Peril

Sometimes I worry that we are at risk of losing our folklore. We are certainly losing a lot of the details of the classics, largely because they are being over-written in the public eye by their adaptation for pop-culture and movies and such.

Don't get me wrong... I don't mean that the original tales are disappearing as such - but *are* they being relegated to those desiccated tomes on researcher's shelves? Presumably, in favour of freshly minted flashy CGI which tells an abbreviated or popularised version of a story, leaving out the gritty detail in the background.

For example... most people these days would likely think of Perseus in terms of defeating the evil Medusa, and fighting the Kraken, and never know that there were some fairly villainous depths to the character... as we will discuss later in this book.

How many people know the part of the Arthurian legends which discuss Ysbaddaden, the chief of the giants? Or Elaine of Astolat, a young noble-woman who was cursed and imprisoned in a tower up the river from Camelot? (Admittedly itself popularised in a Tennyson poem)

Perhaps it's just Western folklore being hit? I don't know. No exclusion intended. Are West African *Akan* folk tales immune? Or the *Jumal* or *Taevataat* tales from Estonia. Greek and Arthurian legends have shown themselves to be movie-magnets, however, so are perhaps walloped a bit more frequently than the stories of *Anansi* or *Kulmking*.

What am I afraid people will lose? Afraid is perhaps too strong a term - but these tales in their earliest forms can be wonderful insights for the cultural and social anthropology of societies which have, for all intents and purposes, disappeared.

Little soap-bubbles replete with meaning floating up through history.

"If you want to tell a story about humanity, then mythology seems to be the best way to do it, if you do it in your own time it looks like it's a political comment on this particular style of government, or this particular class of person, whereas mythology is so universal."
- Stephen Fry (though again, focusing on the Greek)

Folklore is still taught and told frequently in schools, I'm sure... and reading the originals in school is one thing... but the general influence through bombardment with trivialised CGI action, which perhaps just nods in the direction of the tale, tends to relegate that deeper meaning to the domain of the academic.

Perhaps I'm over-stating it. It's a given that new versions of old tales have popped up since those old tales were themselves new. Folklore changes to reflect the people who are telling it - and I guess we can't forget that.

The tales we now consider folklore certainly weren't the original tales told... usually by word of mouth... and these stories have always changed over the ages... but are we at a critical point now where popular culture is over-writing previous understanding at a significantly increased rate? It's an interesting thought.

The Caveats

I need to caveat this book by stating outright that I am not a scholar. I've collected these tales as I've heard them, and the little 'research' I have done is to glean a few interesting tidbits out of the morass of information to include with them. I present them to you for entertainment, and hopefully to spark your interest, rather than as a serious exposition into the origins and etymology of any individual tale.

I've selected antagonists, for the most part. The villains of the piece. They tend to be the focus of the stories, anyway, and they are – quite frankly – a little easier to write about.

These villains have been featured in other books I've written, so if you own one or more of the *Villainy Triumvirate* (Villainy, Combustible Penguins, and As Yet Untitled) series, you'll almost certainly recognise them. I have, however, tried to make them different enough that it doesn't feel like you're reading the same thing.

FOLKLORE

By Rob Mordor

Compiled November 2022

Cover Design by: Rob Mordor

The Villainy Team:
Rachel Gatland, Frances Shingles-Bryant, Adam Charter, Claire Phipps

Facebook.com/groups/TopVillains

THE FOLKLORE

Aswang

If you're Filipino, chances are you know all about Aswang already. If you're not from that neck of the woods, it's a critter that has perhaps dropped under your radar. It shouldn't because it's terrifying, and supremely villainous.

For starters, it's not a single type of critter, but an umbrella term for a range of monsters that shape-shift and tend to prey on humans. They're inherently evil, and really don't have any motives beyond harming folk... and while they tend to prefer the wilderness, they're quite happy living in a city, if they can find somewhere to keep out of the way when they're not hunting. The main varieties of aswang are:

- **The Vampire**: Which uses a long proboscis-like tongue to stab the victim, and drain their blood. They tend to look like beautiful women during the day, and play the long game. They may marry into a family, and then slowly drain the husband of blood before moving onto other family members.
- **The Viscera Sucker**: As delightful as it sounds, this creature uses its proboscis to suck out the internal organs of a victim.

However, only the top half goes hunting. At night, it separates into two halves, hides its legs and lower torso, sprouts wings, and flies around looking for victims. It is particularly fond of eating unborn children.

- **The Werebeast**: Disguising itself as a large dog or feral cat by night, this creature is usually an itinerant labourer or peddler by day. However, when hunting in its beast form, it will travel along the rural roads and hunt those who are walking alone at night.
- **The Witch**: Hurling curses with wild abandon against anyone who has slighted her, this aswang can make you vomit up your own bones, or even weird things like insects. You can spot one of these because their eyes have elongated irises like cats, and reflect images upside-down.
- **The Ghoul**: Subsisting on a diet of human corpses, this creature will generally avoid people, though has been known to attack them just on principle. They mostly live in the wilderness, especially near cemeteries, where they will wait for a fresh burial. They smell vile - their odour can render you senseless - and they have black eyes, and claws to help them dig.

In general, an aswang is more powerful at night than during the day. They will usually take steps to disguise their nature if they are among people... some are remarkably good at it, like the vampire... others - like the ghoul - couldn't pass for human if they tried.

If you want protection against these creatures - according to legend - there are various objects which will help. Almost any holy objects will do the job... as well as general household spices, salt, vinegar, and ash, some sea-side objects such as the tail of a sting-ray, or large crustaceans might also help.

Even urine. It seems they are not partial to wee, or having big crabs hurled at them. Which - realistically - would probably see most normal people off, let alone monstrous ones.

Stories of these terrifying creatures date back to at least the 16th century, when Spanish explorers created the first written record of monster. It was noted that out of all of the monsters in the local bestiaries... it was the aswang that terrified people the most.

Aswang

"They tend to look like beautiful women during the day, and play the long game"

Aqrabuamelu

I know! It's a word that has a Q in it that isn't followed immediately by a U... but it's also a rather terrifying creature that you really don't want to meet on a dark night. It's part man, part scorpion, and a lot more scary that Dwayne 'The Rock' Dibbley.

To understand what this is all about, we have to go back a long way... all the way to ancient Mesapotamia, and the Epic of Gilgamesh.

The Epic of Gilgamesh is an incredibly old epic poem from Mesopotamia, and is regarded by most relevant scholars as the one of the absolute earliest surviving examples of notable literature. It follows the exploits of the fabled king of Uruk, Giglamesh, and dates from the Third Dynasty of Ur (c. 2100 BC).

In the Epic, the Aqrabuamelu are guardians of the Sun God Shamash, and they wait outside the gates of his fortress in the underworld, under the mountains of Mashu... opening the gates for him in the morning as he begins his rounds and closing them after he returns at night.

Gilgamesh met them on his way to Utnapishtim. They are described as having heads that touch the sky, beings of awesome terror whose very glance is death.

They're not just impressive and terrifying doormen, however. They originally served a much darker purpose. According to ancient texts, the Aqrabuamelu were created creatures. Tiamat (primordial goddess of the sea) crafted them to wage war against the younger gods for the murder of her mate Absu.

She built them with the tail and body of a massive scorpion, with the torso, arms, and head of a giant man. She gave them the power of unerring marksmanship, and every arrow they fired from their god-hewn bows would always find their target and cause instant death.

They won many battles against the younger gods, thinning the crop as it were, until Marduk - the dragon god, and patron of the city of Babylon - put an end to it, and had them sent to guard the gates to the underworld. One does not mess with Marduk.

It's at this point that I could start throwing in just about any old random word, and you'd probably have to be a scholar to realise that I'd just made up words like Woffleplutnum and Munglebesh to make the story more interesting... but the whole thing is probably a lot less contrived if you were ancient and originally from Mesapotamia.

The giant scary scorpion men are not without their good points, however. While terrifying, and deadly guardians of the underworld, and merciless god-killers given half a chance, the Aqrabualemu will also sometimes provide warning for travellers who are in danger... presuming they don't look upon you with their death-gaze.

Amazake-babaa

Frequently in folklore, being the nice person will mean that you may be menaced by the monsters, but you're not going to be all that badly inconvenienced by them. You're often the victor in the piece. Not so much with Amazake-babaa, however. You can find yourself on the wrong end of her regardless of how pleasant you might be. She's a horrible monster in a mostly human form, and she spent her nights terrorising the townships of Ancient Japan.

There is a type of supernatural entity in Japan known as a Yōkai. They're spirits, and they're not always villains. The Kanji form of the name Yōkai contains symbols that can also mean 'attractive', and 'pleasant', but also 'calamity' and 'suspicious'... so you're in for a pretty mixed bag.

From a western perspective it might be tempting to think of them as demons, but they're not. Not really. They can really be anything from a benevolent spirit to an annoying trickster, to a horrifying monster with little to no redeeming features. Amazake-babaa likely falls into the last category, because she's certainly not benevolent, and while she may be considered a trickster, the consequences can be catastrophic.

You can't be considered benevolent, for example, if

you are also known as *The Goddess of Chicken-Pox*. Which is an unfortunate appellation, but an apt one. She appears in the form of an ancient hag or crone, and spends her nights knocking on doors of homes on the outskirts of a town.

Not just knocking. She will call out in a child-like voice to ask for *amazake*, a traditional Japanese sweet low-alcohol drink made of fermented rice), as if she was injured, or in some distress.

If someone turned up at your doorstep at 2am and asked for a low alcohol cider, you'd almost certainly tell them to ... well, the polite term is "go away"... but if you were to refuse Amazake-babaa, you will fall ill. The nature of the illness is not discussed in any great detail, but given that she is called *The Goddess of Chicken-Pox*, we can probably put two and two together at this point.

So... you should be nice, and make sure that if someone knocks on your door asking for alcohol, you provide it to them, yes? Well, this is how you know Amazake-babaa is a proper villain.

Even if you say yes, and provide her with the amazake that she clearly wants, she'll make you sick anyway. The only way to avoid becoming ill and covered with horrible pustules is to avoid answering her altogether. Or better yet, find a way to stop her from knocking on your door in the first place.

How do you do that? A sign saying "No Yōkai" is probably going to cause you more problems than it solves... but placing a cedar leaf on your doorway is apparently all you need. I don't know whether you need to nail it there, or wedge it in the door frame... but Amazake-babaa will give you the swerve if you've got one.

Japanese folklore is replete with unusual monsters that will frequently make a western audience double-take, and often go "wut?", but it's a rich and complex culture with a heck of a lot to admire about it.

If you want to get a feel for the unusual, you could certainly do worse than pick up a book of Japanese folklore. Some of the tales are real eye-openers.

Awd Goggie

Yorkshire. You will never find a more wretched hive of scum and villainy, and throughout the eons, children have scrumped from the orchards to the point where poor farmers have despaired.

So what do you do when the local carpet monkeys are clambering into your foliage and depriving you of your Goosegog berries? Barbed wire wasn't a thing back in ye olden times, and large dogs with orange eyebrows were still generally an overseas thing.

No, you had to use cunning to defeat the thieving little hedge-hobbits of t' Dales... and to do this, you tell them of the horrors that await them should they continue to munch upon your unmunchables.

And so we have the likely genesis of a creature called *Awd Goggie*. And strange one this is.

A boggart, a spirit of the forest, and certainly worthy of its home in the beleaguered orchards in the north of England.

Able to take on the form of a giant hairy caterpillar, this creature could clamber among the treetops unseen - and if a wayward child was found unlawfully in possession of a goosegog berry, a rufflefruit, a dinglebower, a mollypecker, or even a lowly apple, Awd Goggie would pounce... at least as much as a caterpillar *can* bounce, and would swallow them whole.

Terminal consumption by a giant fluffy wormy thing would seem bad enough, to be sure... but that's not where the punishment ends... for after a few days the child - still alive - would pass through the digestive system of the enormous fairy-grub, and be... erm... 'reborn' as a sort-of husk which, after a few days, would crack open to expose a mass of writhing filthy maggots... each the size of your thumb, and each bearing the face of the naughty child.

Better, I think, to avoid the scrumpery, and stick to the wild fruits... or the rat on a stick, if you're nominally a city-kid. Scrumping is certainly still a thing in the cities... though perhaps that's not quite the right term when what you're scrumping is televisions.

Awd Goggie would find a city a bountiful place, if it's theft that drives its villainy... but a giant caterpillar in the city might be a bit more obvious than in the countryside... where you might just assume that it looked big because you were closer than you thought you were.

So, did knowledge of the rather terrifying Awd Goggie result in fewer incidents of scrumping?

Honestly, it's almost impossible to tell... but when was the last time you saw a goosegog, a rufflefruit, or a mollypecker? Scrumped to (near) extinction... so I would say it's unlikely to have been all that useful as a myth from a practical standpoint.

Goggie can eventually turn into butterflies... but these were said to be deadly, and extremely rare, as the caterpillar portion of the Goggie's lifecycle could be hundreds, if not thousands of years long.

Al

Armenian folklore is an interesting rabbit hole to go down. It shares a lot in common with the rest of the Caucasus region, between the Black Sea and the Caspian Sea. And Al - admittedly known by several different names throughout the region - is a horrible creature.

While known for a long time in Eurasian folklore, the stories of the Al did not reach European literature until the mid-1800s.

To clarify, that's a capital "A" and a lower-case "L". We're not talking about Artificial Intelligence (AI) here... certainly not from the mid-1800s.

Al isn't just one creature - it's a class of demon, and they prey almost exclusively on women in childbirth. They take the form of old crones... loosely... because I think you'll admit that their description borders on the... well, I think 'unusual' is a reasonable term.

They have clay noses, for some reason. Perhaps to hide the fact that they don't really have real ones, in a very Voldemorty sort of way.

They have fiery eyes that glow in the shadows,

sharp fangs, messy hair, claws made of copper, teeth made of iron, the tusks of a wild boar, and large sagging breasts.

Teeth appear to be very much the aesthetic here. Teeth, fangs and tusks... let alone the claws... this creature is well equipped to be stabby and bitey.

The demon's face is red, and they will carry a self-made reed basket, into which they place their loot.

Now... "loot" to you and I in the context of ancient tales will usually mean gold or jewels... but the Al has a different set of priorities. You see, they will sneak into the birthing area and steal the lung, liver or heart of a woman in childbirth... or who have just given birth.

They will stow these items in the reed bag and will then scarper.

If they cross the first source of water, that's it... they're gone, and there's nothing that you can do to save the poor woman... but if you can catch them and dispatch them before they can cross... well... the tales are a bit confusing, but apparently the woman can be saved.

Um... I'm going to assume through magical means rather than surgery, because... well, ancient surgery tended to stick to things like drilling holes in your head to let out the foul vapours, and re-attaching hearts and lungs would seem to be beyond the ken of most at the time.

When they're not stealing body parts, they can steal a newly born child - though the 'rules' say only within the first 40 days of birth for some reason - and replace that child with an imp.

There are several protections against the Al, according to the folklore. That is, 'apotropaic' (protective) wards, including such methods as charms, prayers, iron objects, onions, and garlic... and of course preventing the Al from reaching the water.

According to Near Eastern traditional tales, the first Al was created by God as Adam's first consort in the garden of Eden, but Adam, being merely a man, couldn't get to grips with the rather chaotic nature of the Al... so it was cast out of the Garden.

This is supposed to explain why the Al and women (technically, Eve and her daughters) did not get along, and why women and young children were targeted by this rejected thing.

Balor

Giants are a staple when it comes to folklore. From the tale of David and Goliath to the Giant's Causeway, to Jack and the Beanstalk... a tale involving a giant will be an enduring one, and often quite exciting. It's pretty clear that the Irish throughout history have loved their tales about giants – and much of their folklore is spectacular and epic. Balor is such a tale.

Balor was the tyrant leader of a race of giants known as *Fomorians*. The Fomorians appear frequently in Irish folklore, and are often monstrous and hostile. Their origins change according to the telling, but they can spring from under the ground, or from across the sea. They were usually gigantic in stature.

Balor was an oppressor of the first people of Ireland, the mortal enemy of the other fae who made Ireland their home.

When Balor was a child, as the story goes, he disobeyed his father and looked directly into a mystical cauldron which was being used by his father's druids to brew a magic potion. This resulted in a magical curse, in which his face was mutated, and his eyes joined together to become one large, putrid, poisonous orb. At first horrified, he soon realised that there were benefits to the curse.

With this eye, he could destroy anything upon which he gazed.

That single eye – a venomous fiery eye – was always covered with seven veils. This is what it took to contain the eye's evil power. As he removed them one by one, bracken would wither, grass would die, timber would smoulder, a dire red glow would spread across the sky, sparks would fly, and the landscape would burst into flame.

Needless to say, this could be a considerable issue if you wanted to, say, stop him from oppressing you by just snicking his oversized head from his gargantuan body. Whole armies could be reduced to charcoal just by a single deadly gaze from an uncovered eye.

As with all such things, however, there was a prophecy. In this particular prophecy, it was said that Balor would be killed by his own grandson. In order to ensure that he never had a grandson, Balor locked his daughter in a tower, and forbid her from seeing anyone.

This doesn't work, and she somehow manages to arrange a booty-call and falls pregnant.

When the child (Lugh) is born, he is whisked away by the sea-God Manannán, before Balor can kill the child, and is raised elsewhere.

Well, you know how this works. We've all heard a good prophecy. Certainly there are enough tales, books, and movies that cover the issue in some detail... and this case is no different. When Lugh comes of age, he nips back to Ireland and leads some pre-Christian Gaelic deities (the *Tuatha Dé Danann*, who have long been enemies Balor) to battle against the Fomorians and kills Balor with a mighty thrust of his magic spear.

Balor's head is severed and set in the fork of a large tree. The tree soaked up the venomous blood that dripped from the open wound, and became a twisted – through very strong – massive tree. Notable, in that it was later felled, and the wood used to craft the spear of a giant called *Fionn* that we shall come to a little later, when we arrive at the formation of the Giant's Causeway.

There are many interpretations (and frankly, versions) of the tale of Balor. Many consider it to be harvest folklore, about the battle between blight and plenty... but it doesn't really matter. Balor is a proper villain, in the traditional sense.

Baba Yaga

Often cast in the role of witch, or child-eating monster, the Baba Yaga figure in 16th century Slavic folklore is normally portrayed as a misshapen old woman who lives in a cottage which is supported by giant chicken legs.

When you hear a phrase like "child-eating monster" then you will generally -quite rightly- assume that we're talking about a villain. Baba Yaga's story is, however, rather more complicated than that.

Depending on the story you listen to, Baba Yaga might be a friend or a foe. She might help you find a missing bride or eat your family. She is one of those ambiguous characters who you can't really take for granted.

Having said that... even if she was a totally lovely old lady in a chicken-leg house who gave you sweets, helped you find your bride, paid your mortgage, and helped you balance your budget... and only ever ate kids once or twice a year... I'd still have to be leaning more or less in favour of her being, basically, pretty villainous.

Baba Yaga first appears in print around 1755, though the oral tradition almost certainly goes back significantly further than that. Baba Yaga is mentioned a couple of times in, oddly enough, a book about Russian grammar by a Russian scientist called *Mikhail Lomonosov.*

In some tales, she's not even a single person - but three sisters, who the protagonist will meet one after the other in that tried-and-true Three Little Pigs format... or the three fates... or three furies... or the three Erinyes (which we'll come to later)... because everything seems to happen in threes.

The three sisters all have the same name, strangely, and this concept was popularised in the work of *Alexander Nokolayevich*, a Russian ethnographer who was known for one of the largest collections of folklore – eight volumes of it, in fact – though possibly a bit harder to read than this meagre book if you're not particularly fluent in Russian.

According to the tale with the three sisters, a hero finds one of the Baba Yagas, and is sent in turn to the second, and the third, each some distance away. The first two are helpful, but the third attempts to eat him. It is only through the blowing of three horns, and the subsequent arrival of an awful lot of wild birds, that saves him – and he flies away on the back of a 'firebird' – which is possibly a phoenix.

The Baba Yaga character was also quite popular in woodcuttings in the 17th and 18th centuries. In some of these pictures, she rides a pig into battle against a crocodile monster... in others she can be seen menacing an old man playing the bagpipes. There is generally some text accompanying these pictures, but they do not seem to form the basis of a story in themselves, so much as perhaps being a 17th century equivalent of a collecting-card game. Medieval witch-based Pokémon, perhaps.

It's an enduring character, particularly in Europe, though starting to be seen more and more in mainstream western media, from graphic novels to computer games to movies... even being mentioned in computer games such as Runescape, or movies like John Wick and the 2019 reboot of the Hellboy universe.

Baba
Yaga

*"When you hear a phrase like "child-eating monster"
then you will generally -quite rightly- assume that
we're talking about a villain."*

Brazen Talos

If you're an aficionado of old movies, you may recall Jason and the Argonauts, from 1963, a stop-motion rollercoaster ride of monsters and mayhem. Foremost in the movie's bestiary was Talos, the giant bronze statue that terrorised the crew of the Argos as they tried to find their way to find the legendary Golden Fleece.

This is all that most people may know of Talos... that small collection of stop-motion scenes in an old movie, as the giant statue serves to protect the treasure of the gods from theft by mortal men.

Talos wasn't made up for the movie, though. Talos was very much a mythological masterpiece a long time before film legend Ray Harryhausen raised his talented hands in anger and brought him to life on the big screen.

Incidentally, while it's made purely for entertainment, and not for historical or mythological accuracy, and end rather abruptly, the 1963 Jason and the Argonauts movie is definitely worth watching if you get the chance. It's usually streaming somewhere.

The Origin Tale

Talos is discussed at length in *Bibliothēkē* - a first-century anthology of Greek myths and legends. Quite interesting are the origin tales - which it has to be said are not all in agreement with one another. The most common tales tend to state that Talos is the survivor of the *Age of Bronze*, where creatures made of bronze stalk the land, and is a member of the Brazen Race... or that he was a living man of bronze built by the god Hephaestus and given to Minos, the King of Crete... or that Talos wasn't a man at all, but was a giant bronze bull forged by Hephaestus and, again, given to Kind Minos.

According to *Argonautica* (a collection of tales from the third century), Talos was an automaton that was used to protect Europa in Crete by throwing large rocks at approaching ships. He would patrol the island's coastline three times daily.

According to the *Suda* (a 10th century encyclopaedia from the Eastern Roman Empire, Talos escaped the Sardinians by hurling himself into a fire, heating himself until he became red hot, and then hugging all of his captors in a deadly embrace.

The movie Jason and the Argonauts clearly took the second point and ran with it - Talos being originally encountered as a giant statue who comes to life when Hercules steals a needle from the Gods' treasure room.

In fairness, the needle depicted in the movie is almost the height of a man, and would make an exceptional spear, so it's not as petty as it might sound. Incurring the wrath of a massive bronze monster because you felt like stealing a regular-sized needle would be silly, after all.

The End of Talos

Talos was built with only one vein, and it ran from his neck, all the way down his body to one of his ankles, at which point it was sealed with a bronze nail. According to the tale, the Argo (and therefore Jason and his crew) were initially driven away by Talos hurling rocks - which is a little different to the movie.

In the tale he wasn't killed by Jason at all... though there are multiple versions of his demise.

- Talos was slain when Medea the sorceress drove him mad with drugs.
- Medea the sorceress deceived him into believing that she would make him immortal by removing the nail.

The nail story is the most prevalent - and certainly the one most like the film. When the nail was dislodged, the ichor flowed from him like molten lead. Interestingly similar to the tale of Achilles, who also had a weakness in his heel/ankle.

Hephaestus was quite the accomplished tinkerer. Given that he was a God, and this was essentially his role, you can certainly appreciate that he should be. He is also said to have created golden women with the knowledge of the Gods, Apollo's chariot, the silver bow of Artemis, Hercules breastplate, and much more.

Brazen Talos

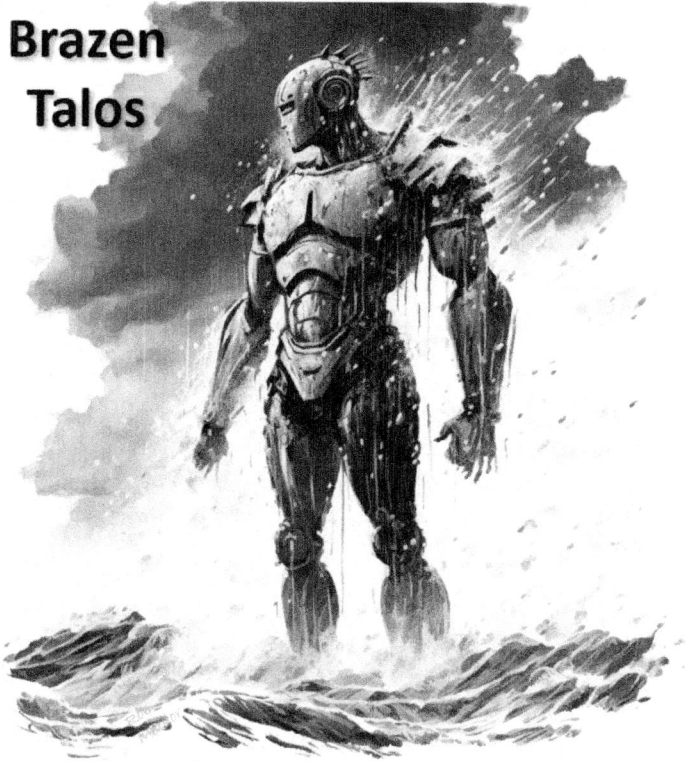

"Talos was an automaton that was used to protect Europa in Crete by throwing large rocks at approaching ships."

Black Shuck

I like dogs. I've never met a dog I didn't like... at least, not after I'd had a chance to think about it. Black Shuck, however, is probably a dog you'd want to be particularly careful about, as it haunts the coastline and countryside of East Anglia, in the East of England.

It is described as jet black with eyes red as coals, and of such a size as to strike fear into the most hardened of men. In the tales the size can vary from that of a large dog, to that of a horse.

Would you rather be stalked by five dog-sized horses, or one horse-sized dog?

Usually, Black Shuck is alone, but sometimes he is at the head of a Wild Hunt - a strange and terrifying event where shadowy figures hurl themselves across the land in pursuit of some unknown beast. The dog is traditionally seen as a harbinger of death.

As far as the tales of Black Shuck go, the first known record of the creature goes as far back as the 12th century, with a report in the Peterborough Chronicle - which recounts one such hunt.

In the 16th Century in Blythburgh, some 100 miles

or so from Peterborough, Black Shuck burst into the church, smashing the doors asunder, and racing up the aisle:

[it] passed between two persons, as they were kneeling uppon their knees, and occupied in prayer as it seemed, wrung the necks of them bothe at one instant clene backward, in somuch that even at a mome[n]t where they kneeled, they stra[n]gely dyed. - Abraham Abrams (1577)

The creature is also frequently seen on beaches and remote areas across the land, sometimes following people, and other times just standing there watching. It has also been found stalking churchyards at night, and sightings continue even into contemporary times.

One woman reports the dog following her for a while when she was walking home from a dance, as late as the 1950s, along a narrow lane.

With the exception of a couple of reports of deaths in churches, and the occasional other rare attack, the beast seems more of a warning or a harbinger, than a clear and present danger... but one of the more curious cryptids, nevertheless.

As for the name... Shuck comes from the Old English word scucca, meaning a devil, or a fiend... so it's not likely to be a bouncy, happy dog, who just wants you to

ROB MORDOR

throw a ball.

Big Bad Wolf (Riding Hood)

From European mythology from the 16th century, the story of Red Riding Hood is known to many. Some versions are fairly tame - others are gruesome in the extreme, but all have one simple characteristic... the Big Bad Wolf.

Wolves had always been considered villains in old European culture, because they were the teeth that lived in the darkness and tended to be rather insistent during the winter months when their usual food was scarcer.

In the story of Red Riding Hood, the wolf has an element of personification. He's intent on eating the young girl Red Riding Hood, and whatever she's carrying in her basket to her grandmother who (for some obscure reason) lives deep in the woods.

Showing an extraordinary level of unnecessary planning, the wolf runs ahead, and disposes of the grandmother. (In some versions, he eats her whole. In others, he simply locks her in the cupboard).

When Red Riding Hood turns up, the wolf puts on a good show pretending to be her. There's the famous "What big ears you have, Grandma!" and "All the better to hear you with, my dear!" interplay before the dénouement.

Again, at this point, versions of the story differ. Most of them end badly for Red Riding Hood, as the wolf leaps out of bed and devours her before falling asleep.

Some versions end there. Others end up with the sleeping wolf being later killed by a woodsman with an axe, or by having his stomach filled with stones and him then being dropped down a well. A joyous child's tale, I'm sure we can all agree.

The sanitised versions, however, involve a last-minute rescue, as Red Riding Hood is saved by the woodsman, who leaps into the home and dispatches the wolf with extreme prejudice.

It's fairly typical for a tale to have morphed over the generations when it is this old, and to have different versions told in different regions. Most of the early tellings tend to be grim ('scuse pun) with the later tellings being the ones that are more child-friendly and palatable.

The message is fairly clear, however. Back in the day the message would likely have been "Keep away from the bloody wolves. They'll eat you." but has morphed somewhat into more of an allegory for Stranger Danger.

However you look at it, the Big Bad Wolf, with his big ears, sharp teeth, and piercing eyes, is an enduring villain, and recognised now across a great many cultures.

All the better to eat you with, my dear.

Big Bad Wolf. (Three Little Pigs)

The story of the Three Little Pigs is very old. The first known written versions were from around 1840, but the story itself is believed to be far older. Bear with me here.

The story begins with the title characters (the rather cocksure oinkers who are, presumably, related) heading out into the wide world to "seek out their fortune".

It is a tale of... in some ways... reaping what you sow. Putting in the effort confers the greatest rewards. That sort of irritating *finoonitar* that parents like to tell their kids constantly in order to make sure they all grow up to be lawyers and doctors.

It follows the 'rule of three' format that many tales do... two failures and a success in this case... which follows the theory that three items, or three elements to a tale, are more satisfying, or humorous, or enduring, than one – and it certainly helps to elaborate the menace of the wolf and the escalating levels of effort that go into protection from it.

The first pig, who has a fairly laid-back attitude

greets the world with a "meh" and throws together a house made of straw. What the heck he thought he would do with a house made of straw is beyond me. Smoking would certainly not have been advisable.

Either way... along comes the wolf, blows it down, and gobbles him up.

Now, **Piggie #2** has a much better attitude. He doesn't build his house out of straw. He uses sticks. Now, had he continued by padding the sticks with cow poo and mud in a sort-of wattle-and-daub arrangement, then we could have considered him something of a local hero... but no. He stopped at the sticks.

The wolf, of course, was not put off by a bunch of sticks, blew the house down, and... well, you get the idea.

Now... **Pig #3** really puts in the effort. He builds his house out of bricks. Presumably this means he crafted each brick from mud and baked them individually in the sun, and laid them on a wood backing, and found a firm, durable cement to keep them locked in place.

There are many logistical problems here, but most of them revolve around the lack of opposable thumbs.

The wolf comes along but can't blow down the

brick house... and trickery fails, so he tries to climb down the chimney, and is boiled - unfortunately to death - by the big pot of water that the pig is boiling in the fireplace.

The third pig subsequently lives a long and happy life, because he's probably also a lawyer and a doctor (because he put the work in. See children, how the world works?), and has a speedboat, and enjoys a round of golf every now and again.

It's the wolf who's the interesting party here. He announces himself with the taunting:

Little pig, little pig, let me come in.

The pigs, of course, are not having a bar of it, but for some reason like to point out that they are hirsute in the face department by screaming back:

Not by the hair of my chinny-chin-chin.

The formalities having been observed, the wolf rejoinds:

Then I'll huff, and I'll puff, and I'll blow your house in.

This interplay has the feel of a ritual, and it's entirely possible that the challenge/response nature of it has some kind of deeper meaning that has been lost through translation and adaptation. It's hard to say.

It surprises me that wolves are known for their huffing and puffing. When you learn about wolves, there is extremely little mention of their ability to huff, or puff. They may "Woooo", but that's about the extent of it.

If anything, they're more bitey than huffy.

Interestingly, given that the origins of this tale are in some doubt, early versions of the modern form of the tale spring from England in the mid-1800s, on Dartmoor[1] in fact, with three little pixies and a fox, rather than three little pigs and a wolf.

The earliest *printed* version of the tale is from around 1840... but there are reasons to believe that it hails originally from far, far longer ago in what is now Norway and Finland, and the huffy part of the wolf villain actually has some meaning.

In old Germanic lore, for example, wolves were responsible for the howling blizzards. Similar comes out of Norse mythology, including the addendum that earthquakes - which could easily bring down dwellings - were caused by *Fenrisulfr*, the Fen Wolf, trying to escape his Earthly imprisonment.

There is all sorts of written guff about how the wolf represents life's challenges, or similar... and I would be among the first to admit that a determined wolf could be a bit of a challenge... but the early origins and nuance have almost certainly been lost to the mists of time... so now we just have a hungry wolf who likes bacon, two particularly lazy pigs, and a mason.

Black Annis

Haunting the East Midlands of England, around Leicestershire, is a terrifying old crone - a witch to some - with steel-blue skin and talons of iron, who feasts upon children and lives in a cave. Her scream would herald her approach, and villagers would draw their curtains and tremble in the dark.

Or she's an old nun who fell from favour and lived the life of a hermit in post-reformation England... depending on which side of the coin you preferred.

The tale of *Black Annis* is thought to go back centuries - with the first recorded references in the mid-1700s... when a parcel of land was being sold, and its proximity to *Black Anny's Bower Close* was mentioned.

Which is fair. If you're buying land, you want to know if there are any monsters living in it. Otherwise, you'd be really quite irritable once you got there and something started eating you.

The monster is described as an old witch, or hag, as above - and she would retire to her cave in the sandstone hills during the day and stalk the lands at night.

You could hear her scream five miles away, and if you lived within earshot, you'd draw the curtains and place protective herbs on all your windowsills. You could hear her teeth grinding as she approached your home, so you knew to keep away from the windows.

The remote cottage windows in Leicestershire are said to have historically been quite small, so that Black Annis could not comfortably reach into the home to snatch away an unsuspecting child... forcing her to grasp about uselessly with the one hand she could still fit through.

Naturally, these were also tales that were told to keep unruly children in line. You dare not misbehave, or - your almost gleeful parents would state - Black Annis would grab you and take your skin for her skirt!

For that's what she did with her victims. She would eat their flesh and tan their skins to make her skirts.

There are several potential origins for the Black Annis tales; from corrupted tales of ancient goddesses to a medieval anchoress - basically a hermit nun - who lived and died in a cave in the Dane Hills, the story of her life being twisted into a tale to terrify children in the anti-anchorite days of the Protestant Reformation of the 1600s.

Either way, many a poor child was no-doubt kept awake by the screaming of foxes, terrified that Black Annis was going to reach her steel-blue arm into their bedroom and grab them in the night.

Black
Annis

"You could hear her scream five miles away, and if you lived within earshot, you'd draw the curtains and place protective herbs on all your windowsills."

Bellerophon

Hubris and arrogance is the downfall of many a popular figure. At some point, the fame and adulation get to them, and they take one step to far, and get cancelled. One of the earliest celebrities to be cancelled - in Greek Mythology at any rate - was Bellerophon.

Bellerophon - according to mythology - was born in Corinth, in south-central Greece. Some tales say that he was the son of Poseidon, the god of the sea. Others say he was the son of Glaucus, the King of Corinth.

Argos

Early in his life, he was exiled (as so many Greek heroes seemed to be. It was almost a rite of passage.) to Argos (not the UK retail store) for murdering someone - though again, details differ according to which tale you're listening to. Either one of his brothers, or some shadowy ill-defined enemy.

Most of the mythology agrees that things got a bit complicated in Argos.

Bellerophon had made friends with *King Proetus* in Argos, *and Queen Stheneboea* took a bit of a shine to him. One day, when the King was off doing something Kingly, the myth states Stheneboea sidled up to Bellerophon and suggested some... extra-curricular activity.

Bellerophon rebuffed her, unwilling to betray the friendship (or risk the ire) of the King, so Stheneboea - in revenge - made up a tale of how Bellerophon tried to ravish her.

King Proetus was absolutely incensed of course, but guests were protected by the gods, and he absolutely could not do anything against Bellerophon himself, so he asked Bellerophon to deliver a secret message to a neighbouring state, where *King Iobates* - Stheneboea's father - ruled.

According to The Iliad (by Homer. 8th century BC) the message read:

Pray remove the bearer from this world: he attempted to violate my wife, your daughter.

The problem was that King Iobates, excited to have a friend of his son-in-law visit feasted with Bellerophon for nine days before reading the message... at which point, Bellerophon was also his guest, and therefore protected in the same way he had been the court of Proetus.

To get around this, he asked Bellerophon to help him with a problem - the horrible monster, the *Chimera*, which had been terrorising his lands.

Pegasus

The Chimera had the body of a goat, head of a lion, and tail of a snake... and it breathed fire like a dragon. It was causing havoc in the countryside, and Iobates assumed that it would kill Bellerophon.

So Bellerophon, unwittingly, set off towards almost certain death - quietly self-assured. On the way, he was advised by a wise-man that he would need to be better equipped than he was, and needed to obtain the flying horse Pegasus to help him defeat the monster.

The wise man advised him to sleep in the Temple of Athena - which he did.

Again, the tales vary - but Bellerophon was either given Pegasus by Athena, or was given a golden bridle, and captured Pegasus by sneaking up on him while he drank at the sacred pools.

Chimera

Once mounted on his flying steed, he took up a lance and struck out to find the Chimera. It took a while, but he found the beast as it consumed cattle in a field.

He struck at the Chimera but was unable to injure it. The creature's skin was too thick, its breath too hot, and the venom from its whip-like tail too dangerous.

He went through several lances and was fortunate not to be killed by its ferocity. However, he had an idea, and briefly flew away to find a large block of lead.

This, he affixed to the front of his lance, and flew headlong towards the savage beast. It spat fire at him, but he rammed the chunk of lead down its throat, where it melted and choked the creature to death.

The Aftermath

Bellerophon returned triumphant to Iobates, but the king refused to believe that Bellerophon had killed the mighty Chimera and assigned him several more quests - which he completed ably.

The king eventually relented, and forgave the warrior, even going so far as to allow him to marry Princess Philonoe and gave him half of his kingdom.

This is where Bellerophon went off the rails a bit.

He decided that - given he had subdued the king, defeated the Chimera, married the princess, and become wealthy beyond all dreams of avarice - he should be considered a God among men.

He took Pegasus and flew to the top of Mount Olympus to demand a seat among the Gods.

Now... the Greek gods were a capricious bunch at the best of times, and having a mortal (or, at least, half-mortal) come to them uninvited and demand to be recognised as an equal was never going to go down well.

Zeus sent a holy gnat to bite Pegasus, and the flying horse bucked, and Bellerophon fell.

He would have been killed by the fall, but Zeus caused a thornbush to grow to cushion his fall - so Bellerophon lived, but his eyes were scratched out.

Zeus took Pegasus and used him as a pack-horse - and once-mighty Bellerophon lived out the remainder of his life in misery, "devouring his own soul" in thoughts of what might have been, had he not been so arrogant as to presume he had deserved apotheosis.

Bunyip

Don't go to Australia. People were never meant to live there. It's full of things that want to kill you. There is so much venom that you could probably squeeze it out of all of the animals and fill an Olympic sized swimming pool. The creatures that aren't venomous will give you fleas. Or drive Holdens. It's horrible, and it's hot.

But if you do find yourself in Australia - having made it through the gauntlet of snakes (Over 100 venomous varieties), octopus (four highly venomous species), spiders (I lost count), and even the platypus (the only venomous mammal) then keep an eye out for the Bunyip.

The Bunyip is a creature in Australian Aboriginal Folklore (It's also a town, but don't go there either) with tales believed to originate in South-Eastern Australia among the Wemba-Wemba people in an area now known as Victoria.

The word translates loosely to devil or cruel/ evil spirit, but doesn't really encapsulate the complexity of the creature's role in the non-contemporary mythology.

While the name comes from the Southeast of Australia, the creature itself is recorded in mythology across the whole of Australia - though variations in the creature's actions and its name do suggest that the migration from one area to another was slow, and the oral tradition has produced some remarkable shifts in cultural representation.

What does it look like?

In general, however, the Bunyip is described as amphibious, mostly inhabiting wetlands, lakes, and rivers. The physical description does have a tendency to be different geographically. This chimeric creature is therefore hard to define in practical terms.

If you narrow things down, consensus seems to place the creature at around 15ft in length (4.5m) and looking more or less like a swimming dog or seal.

The cynical among us might suggest that what the observer has seen, therefore, is a dog or a seal.

However, they also describe a long neck, a sharp serrated jaw, and a small bird-like head. Others say that the head is more like that of a bulldog, only with prominent ears. Some even describe the entire creature as starfish-shaped. Some even say it's a bit like a hippo.

It has a loud roar, reminiscent of the cough/roar of an African lion. It is also said to be nocturnal, so it mostly comes out at night... mostly.

There are plenty of sighting and accounts

throughout the years, but there has been a tendency for any creature which cannot be immediately identified to be classified as "a Bunyip", so who knows? Perhaps we're talking about lots of different cryptids here, each deserving of their own discrete classification.

The first written description of a bunyip was in the mid 1800s, when it was described in the Geelong Advertiser as:

... uniting the characteristics of a bird and of an alligator. It has a head resembling an emu, with a long bill, [...]. Its body and legs partake of the nature of the alligator. The hind legs are remarkably thick and strong, and the fore legs are much longer, but still of great strength. The extremities are furnished with long claws.
- Geelong Advertiser. July 1845.

Why is it notable?
The creature was dangerous to people. It would attack them if disturbed, and would use large claws to slash at them, or would sometimes crush them in a bear-like hug.

Some legends talk about the origins of the Bunyip... it being a man in the depths of history who broke one of the most sacred laws by eating his totem animal. He was then banished by Biami - the good spirit of the Aboriginal Dreamtime - and became an evil spirit himself... surviving by luring tribesmen and their livestock into the water so that he could eat them.

His roar was said to carry for miles, leaving people afraid to enter the water. By night, he would stalk dry land hunting for women and children to eat.

The Mutation of the Myth

Since the 1800s the tale has changed significantly. The name 'Bunyip' came to mean an imposter, or a pretender to a title. It has even been used by political parties to refer to one another. The creature itself became a plant eater, rather than a savage hunter of mankind... and many children's books cast it in a very sympathetic light.

There are a number of horror movies starring the creature, however, so it's clear that it's still seen in some circles as a monster to be widely avoided.

Bunyip

"The cynical among us might suggest that what the observer has seen, therefore, is a dog or a seal."

Canting Wren

A little-known yarn of woe from the people who brought us Old Man of Storr and the Trows... the tale of the Canting Wren hails from the Shetland Islands, around a thousand years ago.

The boulder-strewn beaches of the islands were a great place to fossick for seafood, and shellfish living in the sand and among the rocks. After a hard-day's work, your ancient labourer could make their way to the water-front and rummage up quite a feast if they knew where to look.

These rocks were also frequently home to the wren, a type of bird endemic to the islands, which nests among the boulders.

It was said, however, that it was bad luck to disturb the eggs of a wren, or take them from their nest, because of the Canting Wren, also known as the Heksefugl, a creature which was not actually a bird, but looked like them, and lived among them.

It was, in point of fact, one of the fae - and while it would happily leave you alone if you left the birds alone, if you disturbed their nests, you would be cursed.

It's not all bad news... in fact, some tales tell of people who helped injured birds, and found their shoes filled with coins (from wrecked ships) the following morning.

But if you were cursed by the Canting Wren, you were in for a world of hurt.

- You would be unable to stack stones atop each other. A problem if you were trying to build homes or field-walls.
- Your fires would still light and burn, but would produce no heat, and would not cook your food.
- Any boat upon which you set sail would flounder as soon as you were out of sight of land, and all hands would be lost, unless they cast you into the sea.

How would you know if you were cursed? The creature would appear before you, a large wren wreathed in black, and offer you a choice. Be cursed for ten years or bring someone to the beach to be drowned in your place.

If you chose the latter, you could avoid the rest of the curse, but for two points: You could never again cross open water... which is a bit of a problem if you live on a relatively small island... and you were made aware of the day of your own death... which would occur due to drowning and could not be avoided.

The Canting Wren really pulled no punches, and it does seem to me that a ten-year curse would be rather less of an embuggerance in the grand scheme of things.

I'm not actually sure if the Canting Wren was supposed to be a single creature which would hang about and protect the birds, or whether there were supposed to be several of them living on the Shetland coastlines... but it's an interesting tale, regardless.

While I find the idea of a magical creature who is out there to protect birds quite fun, it's the "or murder someone else" part of the curse that makes it a villain as far as I'm concerned. It would be far too easy for a scoundrel to try to get out of the unpleasant parts of a curse by roping in poor drunken Dave from the farm next-door.

Crocotta

Imagine all the worst parts of a wolf, and the nastiest parts of a hyena. Mix them all up and give it the power of human speech, and you have a Crocotta. Run away.

Spoken of in hushed tones as far back as Greek geographer Strabo and Pliny the Elder between 63 BC and 24 AD, these mythical creatures were taken pretty seriously. Pliny (who admittedly thought hedgehogs used their prickles to pick up apples by rolling around on them) considered them to be a real creature.

I wouldn't put too much stock into Pliny's 'reckons', however. He has quite the reputation for recording nonsense as fact - though he was certainly one of the best-recorded early-adopters who took Natural Philosophy seriously enough to make a career of it.

The Crocotta reportedly lived in the Indian subcontinent, and around Ethiopia and North Africa. They were said to be extremely muscular and strong and had an all-encompassing hatred for humanity - though the reason for this is not reliably recorded.

Their teeth were long and sharp, and they were

said to hunt in packs. Not always people... but people were definitely right up there on their list of preferences.

Crocotta also did not like dogs. That is, domesticated dogs, who they considered to be just as bad as humans when you got right down to it.

Pliny writes:

Among the shepherd's homesteads it simulates human speech, and picks up the name of one of them so as to call him to come out of doors and tear him to pieces, and also that it imitates a person being sick, to attract the dogs so that it may attack them.[2]

So not only would Crocotta attack humans (and dogs) but it would actively, and quite cleverly, hunt them. This speaks of a savage intelligence, rather than mere animal opportunists... making the creatures rather more scary than - for example - a hungry lion.

Byzantine scholar Photius (late 800's AD) further describes them as being immune to humanity's more powerful weapons of the age:

It is as brave as a lion, as swift as a horse, and as strong as a bull. It cannot be overcome by any weapon of steel.

Its eyes were said to be multi-coloured gems, and if

you stuck one under your tongue, you could see the future. Of course, getting the eyes out of something you couldn't kill, and which could tear you apart with ease, makes this a bit of a moot point.

I'm fairly sure no self-respecting Crocotta was going to let you just wander up and lick its eyeball.

One more villainous creature in a world that once seemed full of mysteries. The Crocotta was a creature of terror for over a thousand years before people started to forget the old tales in favour of new ones.

The Sword of Damocles

Fear and trepidation stalk the land like - to paraphrase Blackadder - two giant stalking things. The mythical Sword of Damocles is the memento mori, the terror hanging over success, the existential dread that accompanies... everything.

The actual tale of the *Sword of Damocles* takes place around the 4th century BC. That's quite a long time ago, so obviously it's up for grabs whether any aspect of it is true... I'm guessing probably not... but it entered European mainstream through its recitation by Cicero - a Roman statesman - who used it to popularise Greek mythology.

It's a tale of the limitation of power, or the ever-present threat, literally hanging over us all - and indeed, from where we got the phrase "hanging over us" in reference to danger or threats.

Damocles himself was a courtier to King Dionysius II of Syracuse. He was one of those fawning toadies who grovel and slither to ingratiate themselves with the bigwigs.

We all know the type. Brown-noses, is probably the more common colloquial term.

Anyway, Damocles was in the middle of a rant, which probably went something like:

Ooh, that is a big scepter. All the ladies like a big scepter. Just look at how amazing your throne is, all gold and such. It must be just totes amazeballs to be the King.[3]

Dionysius II basically rolled his eyes and said something to the effect that "It's not all sunglasses and autographs" and offered to swap places with Damocles for a day, to demonstrate. The only rule being that he was not allowed to leave the throne for the duration of the day.

Damocles jumped at the chance, and the following morning, dressed in all his finest robes, he sat upon the throne, surrounded by gold, and jewels, and all the finest food and drink.

He was breathing in all the kingly awesomeness, when he saw something above him that gave him cause for concern. "What," he said, pointing up, "the feck is going on here?"

Dionysius II said, "Oh, in order to make this more realistic, I've hung a heavy, sharp sword above the throne by a single horsehair. I would imagine that a good thump would cause that to fall."

The point being, Dionysius II had not been a paragon of virtue on his way to the top of the ziggurat, and he had made many enemies along the way. The merest misjudgement or ill-timed policy could result in his death, or the toppling of his powerbase.

In short, he had a sword hanging over him the whole time he sat in his throne, and he was never able to forget about it. Never able to enjoy the trappings of power.

The tale itself had power and was handed down from century to century. Chaucer wrote about it in the Canterbury Tales:

Above, where seated in his tower,
I saw Conquest depicted in his power
There was a sharpened sword above his head
That hung there by the thinnest simple thread.
- Chaucer

Various other Roman poets and historians wrote about it. It has been the basis of computer games, books, and was sung about in "The Rocky Horror Picture Show"... among others.

Damocles eventually begged Dionysius II to release him from his agreement, because he could not bear the ever-present threat of the sword, and he realised that the trappings of power came with a cost.

... and it is from here, and the tale of Damocles, that we get a phrase that a lot of you will have heard...

*With great power comes
great responsibility.*

Deimos and Phobos

It's no surprise that many of our celestial bodies are named after Greek and Roman deities, given that the Greeks and Romans technically discovered quite a few of them... and it's a tradition that has continued into fairly recent years.

We've got Saturn, of course, who was the Roman god of generation, plenty, and wealth. Jupiter, who was the god of the sky, and thunder. Mars, who was God of war, and of course 88705 Potato, who was the God of songs about brand new combine harvesters.

Orbiting Mars, of course, we have the two miniature moons Deimos and Phobos.

These two are the sons of Mars (technically, the Greek equivalent, who is Ares) and Deimos was the godling of the dread you get as you await battle - and Phobos was the godling of the terror you feel during battle.

They're pretty-much ignored in the wider pantheon. In a regular family they'd probably have been the scary second cousins who liked to play irresponsibly with fireworks or something.

The main claim to fame for these two is really only to be found in the epic ancient poem The Shield of

Heracles, where ...

Look, this whole thing is cutting back and forth between Greek and Roman mythology, so I'm going to annoy generations of historians and anthropologists and just stick to whatever sounds less bloody confusing...

Phobos and Deimos and Mars and the Shield of Hercules.

So, Mars gets a bit iffy at Hercules, and challenges him to a duel as he was travelling through Thessaly. The poem goes into great detail about the shield, describing it thus:

[its] whole orb shimmered with enamel and white ivory and electrum, and it glowed with shining gold; and there were zones of cyanus drawn upon it.

... there's more, about vine leaves and quivering bronze fishes and such, but there's only so much detail you can really give when what you're ultimately talking about is a bit of metal to stick between you and the sharp thing that your enemy is holding.[4]

OK, it was made by Hephaestus - the god of blacksmiths - so you'd expect it to be at least a little bit fancy... but let's not go overboard here.

Anyway... Mars goes all tooth-gnashy, and Hercules gets all stalwart and dangerously quiet in a *Geralt of Rivia* kind of way.

I won't go into too much detail, but Deimos tries his 'dread before the battle' thing, and Hercules shrugs it off... Phobos does the same thing during the battle, but Hercules couldn't give a rat's bottom.

Mars is ultimately injured, and falls beneath Hercules, but before the battle can result the death of the god of war, Phobos and Deimos swoop in and rescue the old fellow and whisk him off to wherever it is that gods go when they've been soundly trounced by a (mostly) mortal.

The power differential here is supposed to have been quite staggering. Mars was, after all, not just a freaking god, but a freaking god of actual war. I suspect this is a bit like Superman being beaten up by Hefty Smurf, in the grand scheme of things.

Hercules may have been the son of a god, but his mother was mortal, having been seduced by Jupiter (Zeus) turning up pretending to be her husband... when he was, in point of fact, her great-grandfather.

Maybe Hercules stabbed Mars with his Habsburg jaw.

Either way... there you go... Phobos and Deimos... pantheonic hangers-on who squirrelled away Mars right before he had his block knocked off, therefore ensuring that mankind would forever be plagued by war.

Draugr

Icelandic tales tell of Haugbúi, or Barrow Dwellers - undead creatures who haunt the land, spreading mayhem and corruption before them. The tale of the draugr is not a pleasant one.

Born of spite, greed, and the unwillingness to let go of a grudge, draugr are the corporeal remnants of ghosts who remain shackled to their corpses and stalk the Norse lands.

They are described as either nár-fölr (corpse-pale) or hel-blár (deathly-blue) and bring with them a stink so foul that it brings tears to your eyes. Lesser men were known to die from the stink all by itself.

According to the (mostly Icelandic) folklore, these aren't your typical zombies. They aren't mindless husks. They can still think and reason... but they are driven by a relentless need to cause death and destruction wherever they go.

When they can't find a shepherd, they'll butcher the livestock. They tend to haunt the wilder areas.

They can be either:

1. Tied to one specific area, are fiercely territorial, and will kill anyone who trespasses on what they consider to be their land... be it a farm that became

abandoned when they died, or the area immediately surrounding the barrow in which they may be buried.

2. Roaming - such as the draugr of men who once were fishermen, who would stalk the coasts, killing sailors and terrorising coastal dwellers alike.

They have an insatiable hunger and are likely to tear apart any creature which comes into its grasp, and consume it. A draugr might recognise those it knew in its former life, but it no longer holds any special affection towards them, and they are just as likely to be murdered as anyone else.

Worse still, they can also curse those they encounter. To be cursed by a draugr is to become a draugr... and the tales tell of shepherds, or whole crews of fishing boats, found dead, with every single bone broken - basically bags of rotting meat - who would then rise at night, now draugr themselves.

The curse of becoming a draugr wasn't their only ability. They could curse people with terminal bad luck, or with more usual diseases, or could even bring darkness to an area for an extended period.

Furthermore, while they prefer to be about at night, the daylight does not harm them, and the fact that it was daytime would not make you safe.

They were said to be incredibly strong, and

notoriously hard to kill... though the best way to dispatch a draugr varies according to which tale or saga you happen to read.

Wrestling them back into their graves can do it... but good luck with that, given all of the tools of strength and cursing they could bring to bear against you.

Some tales tell of the resting dead (spirits in hallowed ground) rising up to fight any trespassing draugr, and drive them off, before returning to their graves... and the heroes of the tales, if being chased by a draugr, would be wise to run through a church graveyard to acquire a veritable ghost army to aid them.

Some tales tell of draugr who were completely immune to weapons. Others tell of a vulnerability to iron... though iron alone is not sufficient to kill a draugr.

The preferred method is to cut off the draugr's head, burn the body, and dump the ashes in the sea—the emphasis being on making absolutely sure that the draugr was dead and gone.
- Draugr and Aptrgangr in Old Norse Literature (2005)

If worried that a recently deceased person had been cursed, and ran the risk of rising as a draugr...

or that they might harbour grudges towards the living for some reason... certain steps could be taken to assure that the corpse would not rise as the undead:

- Place an open pair of iron scissors on the chest of the deceased
- Drive iron needles through the soles of their feet
- Tie their big toes together
- Brick up the door to the barrow, because the dead must leave through the way they entered and cannot form a new door.

While originally little-known outside of the traditionally Norse countries, recent popular culture has seen many portrayals of creatures which could be described as draugr... from shows like Game of Thrones to computer games like Skyrim.

In 1994, an exo-planet discovered some 2,300 light years from Earth was named PSR B1257+12 A Draugr, as it is orbiting a pulsar in a dead stellar system.

Draugr

"... iron alone is not sufficient to kill a draugr."

Druon Antigoon

Back in the days of yore, before we all got sucked into sedentary lives of excessive ease, and electrical devices, there lived a giant. A villainous Flemmish giant, in a fortress near what was later to become the city of Antwerp.

At this stage, in the early 2nd century, Antwerp (as it is known now) had been settled by the Germanic Franks (this does not mean it was full of German people called Frank.) along the banks of the River Scheldt.

Now, in this era - which was very much still a Roman era - the river was an important route for transporting goods and people from what is now northern France, Belgium, and the southern Netherlands. The only bridge for dozens of miles also crossed the river near Antwerp.

The villainous giant - Druon Antigoon - would guard the river as it slid past Antwerp, and would extort a toll from anyone who sought to pass or cross over it.

Antigoon wasn't just about the toll, however. He'd steal from the passing watercraft, occasionally kill people for sport, and he took a very dim view of anyone who could not, or would not, pay his rather exorbitant tolls.

He would kill the offender, and cut their hands off, and throw them into the river. Being a giant - and therefore quite big - nobody could stand against him... and he did not give second chances.

When not menacing river-travelers, Antigoon would lurk in his riverside fortress, and consume most of the food which had been intended for Antwerp. It was a pretty grim situation for all concerned.

One day, a young Roman warrior, Silvius Brabo, was drifting by; a passenger on a boat on the Scheldt, bound for the coast. The boat was stopped by the giant. Antigoon stood thigh deep in the waters, his mighty arms braced on the prow of the open-topped riverboat.

His voice boomed, "Pay the toll or perish!", and there was much consternation. There were only a few travelers on the boat, and apart from Silvius, they were all fairly poor. The captain of the boat himself was struggling financially, which is why he was taking passengers instead of cargo. It was beginning to look like everyone was going to be killed, and their hands cut off and thrown into the river.

This didn't bother Antigoon too much. He had a lot of money already, but for him it was the principle of the thing. Plus, he quite enjoyed cutting people's hands off.

Laughing, the vicious Antigoon reached for the giant-sized dagger at his belt... but Silvius was not having a bar of it. Picking up his gladius, he struck at the giant as he reached into the riverboat, and cut the massive hand from the massive arm.

Screaming in agony, arterial blood gushing from the wound, Antigoon fell to his knees, and Silvius struck the giant's head from his body... which slid into the waters, dying, and still reflexively clutching at ruined arm.

At the giant's blood-curdling scream, the people of Antwerp looked towards the rover, and watched in awe as Silvius stood on the prow of the boat, picked up the giant's hand, and tossed it in after him.

The waterways were once more safe for those travelling and crossing.

It is said that this is where Antwerp got its name. Evolving over the years from Hand Werpen, meaning to throw a hand... and even to this day the tale is commemorated with a fountain depicting the end of the tale... when Silvius is throwing the hand... water gushing from the dismembered appendage.

The fountain - built in 1887 - celebrates not only the ancient legend, but also the rather more contemporary freeing of the waterways from Dutch tolls, which had been a problem for Antwerp since the 1700s; hampering the city's growth. The Dutch stopped demanding tolls in 1863, without anything needing to be chopped off.

As with most tales of this pedigree, there are several versions with slightly differing details.

Enyo

Greek mythology is full of villains. The tales are positively replete with them, from the upper echelons of power, right down to the most minor of deities. Many may be more malign than Enyo, but you would be hard pressed to find one more bloodthirsty.

Enyo was the Goddess of War. While her brother Ares was the God of War, he tended to prefer the strategy and tactics. He focused on the martial laws and pitting strength against strength in valorous combat.

Enyo was all about the destruction and bloodshed.

If Ares wanted something utterly messed up, he'd send in Enyo, and she'd wander along with her pals Eris (Strife), Phobos (Fear), and Deimos (Dread), and that would be that.

Enyo delighted in the utter devastation of cities, the genocidal rampages, and the brutality of conflict. She rarely took sides, preferring to play both sides against the middle in an ongoing orgy of violent annihilation.

Even when Zeus, ruler of all of the Gods, was fighting the savage monster Typhon, Enyo preferred to stand back and let things run their course, rather than (logically) side with Zeus. This wasn't because she didn't *like* Zeus particularly – though certainly given the reputation of Zeus, this could be understandable – but because standing back and letting things run their course was what would lead to the most violence and destruction.

Enyo's biggest claim to fame was the role she took in the fall of Troy, where she and her cadré of deities oversaw the sacking and ruination of the city. Not content to oversee a victory, she had to oversee the dismantling of the city, its fires, and the grimly riotous behaviour of the victorious soldiery.

The Romans knew her as Bellona, celebrated her officially in June, and her priests (known as Bellonarii) used to self-flagellate as a blood sacrifice to her power – whipping themselves over their shoulders until their backs ran red with blood.

Basically, in Ancient Greece, if you were forced into war, you really only wanted Ares to attend. If you lost, you might die, certainly... but if his sister Enyo showed up, you knew you were in for more than the usual problems.

The Erinyes

Ever heard the word chthonic? It's ancient Greek for basically coming from under-ground... so when someone talks about a chthonic deity, they mean some kind of deity from the underworld. It's a great word that conjures up all sorts of Cthulhian horror. The Erinyes are three chthonic deities.

They're 'furies', a sort-of vengeful creature that inflicts punishment on the deserving (though often also on the undeserving) based on testimony by the aggrieved.

So... if you're a young-un who picks on oldies, or you broke a sworn oath, or you are in some way egregiously insolent... well, the Erinyes will hound you mercilessly.

Depending on which tales you listen to, these ancient deities (more ancient than the Olympian Gods themselves) are variously described as having snakes for hair, dog's heads, coal black bodies, bat's wings, and blood-shot eyes. Which makes them pretty distinctive, in my opinion.

And by ancient, I really mean it. Before the birth of Zeus, Poseidon, and Hades there was the Titan Cronus. Before Cronus, there was Ouranos, his father.

Ouranos was both son and husband to Gaia... but that all gets a bit disturbing, so we'll park that one, and come back to the slightly less disturbing bit...

Cronus and Ouranos had a falling-out, and Cronus castrated his father. The first three drops of Ouranos' blood to fall upon the Earth became the three furies... the chthonic Erinyes.

In all fairness, the removal of a Titan's gentleman sausage isn't the only origin story for these three deities... in some tales they just coalesced from the darkness. In others they were birthed from the disturbance where the air first brushed against the Earth.

As with many of the early Greek tales, there are several different versions, as envisioned by who happened to be writing about them at the time... and they were written about quite a bit.

Their names are generally accepted as being:

- Alecto - of the Endless Anger
- Megaera - of the Jealous Rage, and
- Tisiphone - of the Vengeful Destruction

... and they are recorded as such in Virgil's Aenid, likely based on a number of sources within the ill-fated library of Alexandria, around 29-19 BC.

In Greek literature they enact a terrible vengeance

- enforcing a policy of blood-for-blood - for acts considered to be too far beyond the pale to be ignored... even if those acts were ordered by the younger gods.

Which doesn't give you a lot of leeway really. If an actual capital-G "God" turns up and tells you to do something... it's an incredibly brave and/or foolish person who would refuse. And then if you did do it... however morally dubious the 'it' you did happens to be... the Erinyes might decide they don't like it... so you're in between a New God Rock, and an Elder God Hard Place.

Eventually, they are placated by the goddess Athena, who rather diplomatically offers them the role of protectors rather than punishers, in order to protect her city of Athens.

Initially, they're not too keen, until Athena points out that Zeus still has a big stockpile of the thunderbolts that were used to defeat many of the elder gods... at which point, the Erinyes decide, "Yeah, OK... fair's fair", and adopt a new mantle... one of 'Semnai', or Venerable Ones.

Nevertheless, it remains 'bad luck' to mention them by name, as it draws their attention... something I should probably have mentioned earlier... and sometimes their old habits will flicker back into life just for long enough to dispose of a particularly truculent villain.

The Erinyes

"Eventually, they are placated by the goddess Athena, who rather diplomatically offers them the role of protectors rather than punishers."

Folke Filbyter

Said to reside around 1100 AD, Folke Filbyter is the popularized name of the pagan progenitor of the Swedish Bjälboätten clan.

The Bjälboätten were an Ostrogothian Swedish family that provided several medieval Swedish bishops, jarls and kings. It also provided three kings of Norway, and one king of Denmark in the 14th century.

Folke Filbyter is a retired Viking and appears as a tragic scorned father in the book by the Swedish writer *Verner von Heidenstam* (1859-1940).[5]

The name Filbyter is believed to mean "foal biter" and refers to a man who - rather horribly - castrates colts with his teeth. Please don't try this at home.

In the tale, Folke has returned home to Sweden, weary from many questionable acts during his Viking expeditions. He forms the settlement of Folketuna and begets three sons from a dwarven maid. Alas, he treats her poorly, and two of his sons leave to travel the world.

Folke takes up with the king of the outlaws to increase his wealth, and things in Folketuna become grim and lawless. People live in the dirt, even those at the top of the hierarchy, and squalor is the order of the day.

Folke is also an atheist who has no truck with organised religion, either worshiping the old gods or the new ones, and as well as being openly scathing about it, will happily destroy religious iconography and idols. In the book, this was further evidence of villainy... though opinions may vary on the matter in modern times.

It is, however, a bit of a shock when one of Folke's sons converts to Christianity and gives his newborn child - Filbyter's grandson - to a travelling friar as a way to save him from the lawlessness at Folketuna. An escape, in a way, from the trap of being related to Folke, and all the unpleasantness this entails.

Folke cannot accept that his grandson and heir has disappeared, and so he sets out on an epic quest to find him. Across the land, his decades-long quest is known to Thane and Thrall alike as Folke's Folly.

Eventually, Folke finds his grandson in Upsala. The boy is a grown Earl now in the service of King Inge, and with him are his uncles - two of Folke's other sons - who have become great men in the King's service.

Alas, they have little wish to be associated with an outlaw as unsavoury as Folke Filbyter, and regardless of his quest want absolutely nothing to do with him. He's seen as a bit of a pariah, and very much spurned. The reunion is rather tragic and in an orgy of self-sacrifice, Folke - now humiliated and rejected - exclaims:

The love of your hearts, my children, you cannot give me, and that was all that I ever asked for.

... before he dies.

The story doesn't end here, as it spans several generations, but Folke's role in it is done.

It's all downright grim and unpleasant, and frankly a complex and somewhat unrewarding read. It is, however, considered something of a local classic, and held in high regard.

Folke was not a pleasant person. He was a Viking, with all the unpleasantness that goes along with the epithet. He was an outlaw, and assister of outlaws. He had little respect for those 'beneath' him and manipulated many to his own ends.

He may come to a tragic end, and be seen as something of a tragic figure, but ultimately, he's a villain from the start. In 1927, a statue to Folke Filbyter was constructed by noted Swedish sculptor Carl Milles in Linköping Ostergötland.

Flatwoods Monster

Let's set the scene. It's West Virginia, USA, 1952. Red Planet Mars and Radar Men from the Moon have been showing in the cinema. World War II has ended, and the Korean War is raging. Tensions are heightened. UFO sightings are going through the roof, and three boys are out at night taking a walk in the countryside.

There's a flash of light overhead. The boys are startled, but they watch as the light plummets towards Earth and land in the property of a local farmer.

Absolutely aware of the tales of spacemen and flying saucers, the boys run to their auntie's nearby farmhouse and tell her what they saw... so several of the lads, and a US Guardsman brave the frigid night to go and check out the landing/impact site.

Thinking that they would get a good look at the site from the top of a nearby hill, the group ascend, thinking that they would be looking down on a crash site of some kind of alien vehicle, or at least a small crater from a meteor.

Instead, as they crest the top of the hill, they see a pulsating red light right where they're about to walk. Something else has ascended the hill before them.

The guardsman trains his torch on the pulsating light, and in front of him is a ghastly shape. Standing around ten feet tall, it had a bright red face, with glowing orange eyes. Around the face is a large fringe of material or skin , pointed like a leaf.

Whatever it is, it's a dark green colour, and it hisses as the light falls upon it, and darts towards the group in an apparently aggressive manner.

The guardsman screams, drops his torch, and the whole group turns and runs as fast as they can back down the hill like the very hounds of hell were nipping at their heels.

After the incident, the group said that they'd smelled a "pungent mist" and felt nauseated after the event.

Subsequent investigations turned up no sign of the monster... though a strange 'skid' site was found in the field, and a strange gummy deposit which UFO enthusiasts claim was proof of an alien visitation.

Of course, it could just be proof that lots of weird stuff happens on a farm... and certainly the Powers That Be declared that the sighting was nothing more than a meteor, followed by a plane's navigation light, and the guardsman misinterpreting the shadow of a barn owl on the hilltop.

Giant's Causeway

Ireland is a land of magic and myth, and in Scotland they're spoiling for a fight. The story of Fionn the Giant is ancient, and explains the rather pleasing geological formation known as The Giants Causeway.

The Giant's Causeway is an area of interlocking hexagonal basalt columns, the result of an ancient volcanic fissure eruption. It is located in County Antrim on the north coast of Northern Ireland, and is thought to be around 60 million years old.

Fionn was a huge giant. He lived on the Irish coast, and went about his business doing gianty things, as one does. One day, as he's chilling out at home, there comes a knock to the door of his keep. It's a messenger.

Before we get too far into this, the tale is old and has a few versions. The name of the primary protagonist shifts a bit depending on where and how the tale is told... Finn or Fionn... and other details vary. The tale is based on legends likely going back to between A.D. 700 into the 1200's.

The exhausted messenger states he has travelled all the way from Scotland, and that Fionn has been challenged to a duel by Benandonner, a huge Scottish giant.

Only one can prevail, and the other was to be cast into the sea to drown.

Which is not very neighbourly, but when you get right down to it, giants aren't really known for their sweet temperaments... otherwise "Fi Fi Fo Fum" would be a chant about playing with kittens, rather than grinding bones and making bread.

Fionn was pretty sure he was the biggest and fiercest giant. He has good armour, and strong weapons, and a shield carved from the wood of the ancient tree that absorbed the venom of the evil Balor... but uncertain as to how to get to Scotland, he decided to hurl rocks into the water to build a causeway from Ireland to the Scottish coast, whereupon he would smite Benandonner.

Benandonner heard that this was happening, and started building the causeway from his end, so that they would meet in the middle.

The work was back-breaking, even for a giant, as each hurled stone after stone into the turbulent waters... but eventually, the causeway was completed.

Alas, Benandonner - tired beyond belief - had fallen asleep on the Scottish coast, and so Fionn was able to approach him without too much difficulty.

However, when he got there, Fionn was terrified. Benandonner was enormous. A giant of such size and raw power that Fionn knew that in a fight to the death, he would lose... and lose quickly.

He ran back across the causeway to his keep, and bolting the sturdy oak door behind him, he explained this to his wife.

Any normal person might have considered braining Benandonner with a basalt column... but Fionn was either (a) too honourable, or (b) too stupid.

His wife wasn't stupid. She knew that no oak door was going to keep out a giant the size of Benandonner... so she thought for a moment, and then started tearing up sheets.

She told Fionn to dress in them - effectively the nappies and swaddling clothes of a baby - and had him build a large log cradle, and go to sleep in it by the keep's fireplace.

Indeed, the following morning, Benandonner charged across the causeway, intent on finding Fionn and ending him. Kicking open the door to Fionn's keep, Benandonner snarled and shouted for "the coward Fionn" to come and meet him in mortal combat.

Fionn's wife appeared and shushed him, saying that Fionn was currently out, but please don't wake the baby.

Benandonner took one look at the sleeping Fionn in the cradle and thought "Good lord... if that's the size of his baby, how big must Fionn be?!" - and with this terrifying thought, he ran back across the causeway, tearing it up behind him.

The place now known as The Giant's Causeway is a coastal area in Ireland where hexagonal pillars of rock were formed by volcanic activity. It is where Fionn is said to have started to build his section of the causeway.

Gnome

A gnome is a mythological creature and diminutive spirit in Renaissance magic and alchemy. It is generally defined as a small humanoid that lives underground.

You're probably more familiar with the rotund little ceramic lawn ornaments, with the little red hats, who occupy a variety of professions in a garden. Many people have had one or more of them.

I had one, with a little yellow waistcoat, leaning against a Pohutukawa Tree looking smug. That is, until a rogue car failed to take a corner, bowled over my garden wall, decapitated my gnome, and smashed my tree. He didn't look quite so smug after that.[6]

Gnomes haven't always had such a wholesome history, however. Their PR manager was originally quite lax, and they were portrayed rather differently than they are today.

First Glimpses

The word comes from Renaissance Latin gnomus, which first appears in A Book on Nymphs, Sylphs, Pygmies, and Salamanders, and on the Other Spirits by Paracelsus, published posthumously in Nysa in 1566.

Paracelsus was a Swiss physician who lived in the 1500s. The name 'Gnome' likely comes from the Greek γη-νομος which translates roughly into Earth Dweller, but this is largely conjecture.

He describes them as two spans high, very reluctant to interact with humans, and able to move through solid earth as easily as humans move through air.
   - Lewis, C. S. (1964). The Discarded Image - An Introduction to Medieval and Renaissance Literature. Cambridge University Press

That's an interesting concept in and of itself. Why don't they therefore fall through the Earth until they reach the magma, and then burn up? Maybe they do, and this is where we get coal from... but if they can walk back and forth in the earth as easily as we walk in the air, the implication is that they'd move up and down in it as easily as air too.

The physics of this - mired as they are in mythology - are probably moot... but this is the sort of mentally peripatetic nonsense that keeps me awake at night.

I digress.

For a while - mainly during the 18th and early 19th centuries - the term Gnome was synonymous with Fairy. They were described in many texts as quite friendly guardians of treasure:

The Earth is filled almost to the center with Gnomes or Pharyes, a people of small stature, the guardians of treasures, of mines, and of precious stones. They are ingenious, friends of men, and easie (sic) to be commandded (sic).

- Nicolas-Pierre-Henri de Montfaucon de Villars, the abbot of Villars (1670). Comte de Gabalis

On Being Sidhe or Fae

Fairies, however, were considered to be distinctly amoral. Not bad as such, perhaps, but alien and arcane and hard to understand. They also encompassed a wider range of creatures than the Tinkerbell style Disneyfication we associate fairies with today. Fairy folk included goblins and dwarves and boggarts and the like.

One moment they were your best friends, bestowing unimaginable gifts and benefits upon you. The next, they were being unimaginably cruel and destructive... and not really understanding the difference between these two states - like the very concept of good or evil was alien to them.

The Red Cap

The Gnome was also originally the Red Cap, a murderous creature - goblinesque - who lived at sites of great woe back in the dark days of the Anglo-Scottish conflicts of the 1700s.

Dwarves are almost always depicted as having Scottish accents. Where this started is anybody's guess, but it's an interesting phenomenon.

I always imagined gnomes as sounding like they come from the West Country, gargling wurzels and sounding all Pertwee at us. (This is perhaps too-niche a reference?)

Their subsequent relocation - mythologically speaking - to the Anglo-Scottish border suggests that perhaps they could compete with the Dwarves for the right to sound Scottish.

I must stop digressing.

Anyway... *Red Cap's* hat was red because he dipped it in the blood of the dead. He is described as:

A short, thickset old man with long prominent teeth, skinny fingers armed with talons like eagles, large eyes of a fiery red colour, grisly hair streaming down his shoulders, iron boots, a pikestaff in his left hand, and a red cap on his head.

- Henderson, William (1879). Folklore of the Northern Counties of England and the Borders (2nd ed.) W. Satchell, Peyton & Co

While this sounds like one individual, other works describe the Red Cap as a class of malevolent spirit rather than an individual. Sounds pretty Gnomey to me.

Later in this book we look at the *Red Cap Powrie*, which is likely to stem from this creature.

Modern Gnomes

As with everything, modern re-tellings, computer games, contemporary novels, and movies totally re-write the history of Gnomes, the same way they re-wrote elves and fairies.

The Garden Gnome version is a popular one - a Disneyfied McGnome of little depth compared to the Grimm and grizzled definitions and descriptions of centuries passed.

Other descriptions as follows:

1. World of Warcraft (1994-present) describes them as an exile race, having irradiated their home city of Gnomeregan using unholy technology to drive away enemies.
2. The Harry Potter franchise (1997-2007) gnomes are pests that inhabit the gardens of witches and wizards.
3. The Chronicles of Narnia (1950-1956) see gnomes used as slaves by the Lady of the Green Kirtle until her defeat, at which point they return to their underground realm of Bism.
4. In the works of JRR Tolkien (1914-1973) gnomes are generally tall, beautiful, dark-haired, light-skinned, immortal. They

tend towards violence and have an abiding
love of the works of their own hands.

Gnome

"Not bad as such, perhaps, but alien and arcane and hard to understand."

Gelert The Dog

I first heard this legend when I was a nipper, and it really wound me up. Prince Llywelyn the Great struck me as the biggest bloody idiot ever to grace the Welsh countryside, and regardless of his importance to Welsh history, I'll always consider him a rotter.

It's the 1100s, and Prince Llywelyn is a bit of a fan of hunting. Most royalty is at this point, if they're not drinking or wenching themselves to death, and Llywelyn has a great many hunting hounds. Big wolfhounds that he used to summon with his horn before setting out on a hunt.

He had a favourite, of course. Gelert, the enormous wolfhound. A bit rough around the edges, but a more loyal animal you would never find. He had been with Llywelyn since being a puppy and was rarely from his master's side.

Gelert was the only hound that was allowed to live inside Llywelyn's castle. All of the other hounds lived in open kennels around the wider estate.

One morning before a great boar hunt, Llywelyn blew his horn, and hounds came bounding out from every corner of the grounds, eager to join him. The prince was a little disappointed not to see Gelert among them... but he was hosting nobles from other parts of the realm, so could not delay. They set off for the hunt.

Llywelyn had left his infant son at home in his nursery with a nanny, and a few servants.

The hunt lasted for the better part of the day, and when Llywelyn eventually got back, he was exhausted. He bade his visitors farewell as they returned to the guest wing and went to see if he could find Gelert in the castle.

As he approached the gates, the enormous shape of Gelert the wolfhound burst free, wagging his tale and bounding with joy but... as Llywelyn noticed... he was covered in blood.

Llywelyn was worried. All of the servants appeared to be absent. Something had chased them off. Horrified, and worried for his son, Llywelyn rushed inside to the nursery.

There he found the walls spattered in blood; the cradle upturned. The same blood that was smeared all over his wolfhound. Gelert 'woofed' behind him, wagging his tail.

In a fit of rage, Llywelyn pulled his sword and stabbed Gelert through the chest, screaming in anger at him, as the poor dog died to his blade.

As his shouts died, he heard the cry of an infant. Dropping his sword, Llywelyn threw aside the cradle, and there was his unharmed child. Beside the unharmed child was the corpse of an enormous dire wolf, which had somehow made its way into the nursery.

It had clearly been dispatched by Gelert before it could harm the child, after it had frightened away the servants and the nanny.

Wracked by remorse, Llywelyn carried his now dead wolfhound outside, buried him in the middle of his estate, and placed a large stone over the grave so that all would know the story of Gelert, the brave and loyal wolfhound.

Llywelyn went on to become a dominant force in Wales, forging peaceful inroads with the English, and was eventually crowned King of Gwynedd, and eventually ruler of all Wales. I still don't like him.

- As a point of clarification: While the tale at its most basic (Huntsman, loyal dog, endangered child) goes back a very long way, the version with Gelert and Llywelyn is much adapted by a chap by the name of Pritchard in the late 1700s, to help draw business to his tavern. Nevertheless, it remains an enduring tale.

Gelert the Wolfhound

"A bit rough around the edges, but a more loyal animal you would never find."

Headless Horseman

When people think "Headless Horseman", most of them will think of America and the Washington Irving's "Legend of Sleepy Hollow" story from 1820 (Or various movies and TV series and books based on the tale) Many will be surprised to learn that the tales of headless horsemen are not just a US phenomenon.

The US Version

Sleepy Hollow's tale is about a Hessian soldier (Hessian's being German soldiers hired by the British forces in the late 1700s) who was killed during The Battle of the White Plains in 1776.

Legend has it that his head was 'removed' by an American cannonball, and his headless body was buried in the Old Dutch Church of Sleepy Hollow... from which his rather unpleasant ghost arises periodically to go in search of his head.

I was genuinely surprised to learn that Sleepy Hollow is a real place. Turns out it is not only real but is parked right next to the moderately bustling New York City. Perhaps not so sleepy anymore... though back in pre-Independence America, it most likely was quite parochial.

The Irish Version

In Ireland, the horseman is the dulachán, or dark

man. He actually sounds a bit nastier than the US version, because he wields a whip made from the spine of a murdered man. He either rides a black horse, with his head under his arm, or drives a black carriage, with his head on the seat beside him.

When he stops riding, and calls out a name, the person whose name he calls immediately dies.

In some versions of the story, he can be repelled by gold... so if you happen to be carrying a large gold object, you can place it in his path, and he will run away.

I guess I could hurl my wedding ring at him... but the wrath of my wife might be worse than the wrath of the dark man.

The Scottish Version

On the sparse Isle of Mull of the Inner Hebrides, the tales tell of a man called Ewen, who was once a contender for chief of the local clan. He was beheaded in battle - as was his horse - and now he and his headless horse haunt the island.

... though if I'm honest, I'm not sure how he steers it.

Gawain and the Green Knight

In this Arthurian era tale, the knight Sir Gawain is challenged to a game of sorts by a mysterious green knight who appears in King Arthur's court upon a mighty green horse.

This involves the knight challenging Gawain to hit him with an axe, on the promise that the blow will be returned a year and a day later.

Gawain snicks the knight's head off with the axe, and everyone assumes that will be the end of it. However, the now headless green knight picks up his head, climbs up on his green horse, and - with it under his arm - demands that Gawain meet him a year hence for the blow to be returned.

It's an interesting - if unusual tale, and perhaps worthy of a proper telling - but does not result in a haunting, so much as a lesson to Gawain.

Herla's Fairy King

Never deal with the fairy folk, because even if you think you're onto a good deal, they'll sucker you right in with their mercurial ways, and the next thing you know you're up to your knees in weird curses, and it's three-hundred years later, and your cat has evolved to be the only other intelligent life-form on the space-ship.

So... here is King Herla - in a tale first recounted in the 12th Century.

Herla was one of the earliest British kings, several hundred years before the tale was first recorded, and around the area now known as Herefordshire, in the west midlands of England.

The king was arranging for his wedding celebration, and he should have known better than to let in the stocky dwarven figure wearing resplendent hunting garb, astride a pony-sized goat - who claimed to be a King of the Fairy Folk.

I mean, don't get me wrong... you don't want to annoy them by being rude either... but there are supposedly ways and means to disarm one of the fae who pops over and casually asks to attend your wedding.

So when the Dwarven Fairy King said "I will attend

your wedding, if in a year, you attend mine!", you should find a nice way of letting him down, rather than thinking about all the presents and such.

Still, Herla agreed, and on the day of his wedding, the dwarven king and his retinue arrive at the castle. They lavish many gifts upon the married couple, and indeed, turn up with gold plates and silk tents, so that the wedding is rather more grand than it was going to be. A jolly good rousing time is had by all.

The next day, the fairy-folk are all gone with nary a trace.

All is well for a year. King Herla and his new wife abide well, and their small kingdom is plentiful and peaceful... something quite rare in the wider Britain at the time.

Then the Dwarven Fairy King arrives, once more astride his pony-sized goat, and says "A year has passed, and my own wedding approaches. Will you and your retinue come feast with me?"

Naturally, the King agrees, and he and his court follow the dwarf back to his small kingdom in the nearby mountains, passing through a crevice in the rocks to get there.

The revels last three full days. There is feasting, singing, dancing, and presents aplenty. King Herla and his court are amazed at the generosity of the Fairy host, and when it finally becomes time for them to leave, they are weighted down with gold, and hawks, and hounds, and the finest longbows, and so forth.

To King Herla, the Dwarven Fairy King gives a special present. A young bloodhound, which he places on the King's saddle as they eventually file back out through the kingdom's narrow entrance, with the warning words "Stay on your horse, good King. Do not dismount before the bloodhound, no matter what. The bloodhound must dismount first, of his own accord!"

Thinking this quite odd, but nevertheless thankful, King Herla thanks the dwarven King, and they bid their farewells and return to Herla's kingdom.

As the men travel back towards the castle, they are confused by the state of the road, which is in poor repair. They come across a farmer and ask him for news of the Queen.

The poor man is flummoxed. He barely understands a word of any in the King's retinue, for he was a Saxon, and did not rightly speak the King's Tongue. Eventually, they work out that... well, it wasn't encouraging.

There was, it seems, a King Herla in legend, but he and his men all disappeared after following a Fairy King into the mountains, and was not seen again, these hundred years hence.

The bloodhound had not dismounted the King's

saddle, but several of the King's court had forgotten the dwarf's warning in their shock, and dismounted. The instant their feet touched the ground, they aged instantly and turned to dust.

King Herla began to understand the nature of the curse that he and his men now appeared to be under.

For centuries hence, the Host of Herla were known to haunt the night in Hereford. They would appear without warning, and dash at great speed from horizon to horizon, in search of something unknown. Sometimes they were seen in the dark just sitting atop their horses, staring sadly into space, as if held in some kind of trance. Sometimes they would just wander aimlessly through the night.

Thus was born the legend of The Great Hunt.

They had become less than men, but more than ghosts.

It is said that the curse ended during the reign of King Henry II, with two prospective endings discussed:

- The first, when after centuries Herla lost faith that the bloodhound would leave his saddle, and the whole host simply stepped off their horses and disappeared into the dust of Hereford forever.
- The second, where the host had become

fully corporeal, and were seen in broad daylight, with no sign of the bloodhound on the King's saddle, as they rode away - restored to proper life - to some unknown fate.

Presumably the moral of this tale is to promote that One should distrust the elder races, and the fairy folk... that even a mighty king could be brought down by their unworldly and unfathomable nature.

Jenny Greenteeth

Known primarily around Liverpool and Lancashire in England is the villainous and vicious creature known as Jenny Greenteeth, who waits just beneath the surface of brackish water to haul in the unwary.

She is usually described as having pale green skin, green teeth, very long green locks of hair, long green fingers with long nails, and she was very thin with a pointed chin and very big green eyes. Green being very much a theme here, as you can tell.

Given that she's all green, the fact that people mostly notice her teeth should be quite telling, as far as these tales go... and the mythology has been around for a very long time - with even modern parents in the Northwest of England invoking her name in order to get children to behave themselves.

- Don't go near the water, or Jenny Greenteeth will get you.
- If you don't brush your teeth, Jenny Greenteeth will get you.

It is also the common name for the pondweed, or duckweed, that grows over small bodies of water - the weed supposedly being her hair - and which can present a danger to those who are not paying attention.

The concept of a water hag with malevolent intent is not unique to the Northwest of England of course... the Jenny Greenteeth creature is quite similar to the Japanese Kappa, Australia's Bunyip, or the French Melusine.

Even in the Northwest of England there are minor variations on the name.

There's no clear origin story. It is likely that the tales sprang from the dangers of still water, the mats of duckweed that potentially hid them, and then entangled those who fell in.

Jenny Greenteeth is likely the inspiration of Meg Mucklebones from the Tom Cruise movie Legend (1985), and Jenny Greenteeth from the Sir Terry Pratchett novel Wee Free Men (2003) - among other numerous references.

Jack Spriggins and the Enchanted Bean

Many a child has shivered in delight when their parents intoned the opening lines of the infamous quatrain "Fee, Fi, Fo, Fum... I smell the blood of an Englishman." - but what are the origins of this dramatic tale of giants and magical beans?

For those who have been living under a bushel, I am of course talking about Jack and the Beanstalk, a tale - and a giant villain - presumably as old as the hills from whence it came.

And whence it came, of course, is England... except... maybe it isn't.

If you're one of the few folk who've never heard the story... there are plenty of modern variants, but here's the precis version without most of the bells and whistles:

Jack and the Beanstalk: A Summary

- Jack is a poor lad from a poor family. He goes to town to sell the family's only cow so they can buy some food. Instead he's given a 'magic bean' by a mysterious stranger.
- His parents are very angry with him, and throw the bean away. Overnight it grows

into a huge beanstalk reaching up above the clouds. Jack climbs it, and finds himself in a realm in which an evil giant lives, in a massive castle.

- He raids the castle , and steals a goose that lays golden eggs, and some other stuff. The giant wakes, and chases him. Jack climbs down the beanstalk, cuts it down, and the giant falls to his death.

- The family now have a goose that lays golden eggs, and everyone's happy. Obviously except the giant... who is a big sticky puddle on the landscape.

Themes

It's a type of tale that follows a very specific theme... young protagonist, powerful villain, and theft. Each type of tale is categorised by researchers, and these are called a Tale Motif. They're each given categorisation code to identify them.

All tale-types in the index are prefaced with either "AT" or "ATU" to indicate whether they are an original tale-type outlined in Aarne and Thompson's 1928 or 1961 index or whether they have been re-organized or created by Uther in the new 2004 index, respectively.

Now... you might be sitting there going "WHY?!" - but it's actually useful to group similar stories together, because it can help you to piece together themes, identify similar narratives, and track the origin of a tale through time, even if it changes a little with every telling due to the oral and written traditions of the various ages and cultures through which it passes.

The Tale Motif of Jack and the Beanstalk is AT-328 "The Treasures of the Giant" and its origins could go back as far as 2,500BC.

There are sub-categories as well, and each may share part of a theme with another, but that gets convoluted, so we'll stick to the basic classification here. (For context... Rapunzel is AT-310, Hansel and Gretel is AT-327a, and Little Red Riding Hood is AT-333)

The Tale Through the Ages
Over four thousand years is an extra-ordinary claim... but the proto-Indian roots of the story, as tracked through the Motif, (and research from Durham University and the Universidade Nova de Lisboa) are compelling. This could genuinely be one of the oldest 'fairy tales' still popular in the modern world. Which is undeniably fascinating.

Further reading: BBC (20 January 2016). "Fairy tale origins thousands of years old, researchers say". BBC News. Retrieved 20 January 2016.

Among the earliest of the recorded 'modern' tellings that we would likely recognise as Jack and the Beanstalk is "The Story of Jack Spriggins and the Enchanted Bean" which was published in 1734 by J. Roberts in the second edition of the publication "Round About Our Coal-Fire" - a book of collected tales.

Since then, of course, it has become remarkably popular, and has resulted in movies, books, and even a Disney cartoon in which Donald, Mickey, and Goofy find themselves at the top of the beanstalk.

As for the famous quatrain that most people associate with the story of Jack and the Beanstalk... it first appears in a slightly different variant in a pamphlet in 1596 called Haue with You to Saffron-Walden - written by Elizabethan playwright Thomas Nashe.

Fy, Fa and fum,
I smell the blood of an Englishman

It's not until 1890, and the works of Australian folklorist Joseph Jacobs that we get the 'modern' version of the quatrain:

Fee-fi-fo-fum,
I smell the blood of an Englishman,
Be he alive, or be he dead,

I'll grind his bones to make my bread.

... though remarkably similar variants go back as far as 1711.

Let's face it... anyone who goes around chanting this in deep sonorous tones, and grinding up bones to make bread, is a villain of the first water.

The giant is a villain of course, rather than a simple victim of burglary by Jack, largely because of his history of raiding the lands beneath, and making meals of stolen oxen and children. This is something that is missed from a lot of the later 'child-friendly' versions of the tale.

Even in the Disney version of the story, the giant had stolen a magic harp that bestowed prosperity on the land, so everyone was starving and poor.

The portrayal of the giant as a villain does give Jack some legitimacy as a hero, because otherwise he's just some guy who climbed a particularly leafy ladder and nicked some big guy's medieval equivalent of a flat-screen TV.

It also goes some way towards excusing Jack's frenzied dispatching of the giant by chopping down the beanstalk as the giant descends. Stretching the burglary metaphor somewhat... if you pushed over a ladder after committing a burglary, as the homeowner was descending it to chase you... well, that's probably going to be called murder.

The giant has become a villain that caused young children to gasp in terror as you told the tale to them in the half-light of bedtime, using all the scary voices, and claw-handed "I'm going to get you" gestures.

Whatever version you've heard, and however you've been exposed to this tale, it's certainly one of the classics, and if it is genunely over 4,000 years old, it's one that has endured for almost two-thirds of the time that mankind has had written language.

John Trundle's Dragon

Before there was the tabloid press, there was John Trundle and his pamphlets. Trundle (1575–1629) was a publisher and bookseller in London, England, and he loved to release pamphlets. In 1614 he had news he wished to share about a dragon, terrorising Sussex.

His pamphlet had an unusual headline:

True and Wonderful: A Discourse relating a strange and monstrous serpent (or dragon) lately discovered, and yet living, to the great annoyance and divers slaughters both of men and cattell, by his strong and violent poison, in Sussex two miles from Horsham,in a woode called S.Leonards Forrest, this present month of August, 1614. With the true generation of serpents.

... because "DRAGON EATS PEOPLE IN SUSSEX!" just wasn't going to cut it, apparently.

Now... the folk of the western side of Sussex perhaps had a bit of an unfair reputation as credulous rural types, but reports of dragons in the area weren't uncommon, oddly... even though the forest in question was by no means a particularly large one - and perhaps not large enough to accommodate something as surly and noticeable as a dragon... but nevertheless, it was described as:

...reputed to be nine foote or rather more in length, and shap't almost in the forme of an Axeltrée of a Cart, a quantity of thick|nesse in the middest, and somewhat smaller at both ends, The former part which he shootes forth (as a necke) is sup|pos'd to be an elle long, with a white ring (as it were) of scales about it, The scales along his backe séemes to bée blackish, and so much as is descoured vnder his bellie ap|peareth to be red, for I speake of no nearer description then of a reasonable ocular distance, for comming too neare it, hath already béene too dearely payd for, as you shall heare hereafter.

... and whether it has feet or not is disputed, because some 'witnesses' said it had big feet, and others said it slithered like a snake.

So we're not talking about a gargantuan mountain-dwelling layer-of-waste here... though if you came across a cat that was "nine foote or rather more in length" it would certainly be brown-trousers time.

Also, for those wondering, an 'elle' is approximately 18 inches. For those still wondering, 18 inches is approximately 45.7cm. For those still wondering, that's roughly 91.4 million beard-seconds.

Clearly, the creature sounds dangerous, which is further explained as follows:

He will cast his venome about foure rodde from him, as by woefull experience it was proued on the bodie of a man and a woman comming that way, who afterward was found dead, being poyson'd and very much sweld, butnot prayd vpon. Likewise a man going to chase it, and as he imagin'd to destroy it with two Mastiue Dogs, (as yet not knowing the great danger of it) his Dogs were both kild, and he himselfe glad to returne with hurt to preserue his owne life.

And so now it squirts poison to kill people... with "four rodde" being approximately 66ft, or a touch over 20m. That's roughly 66.6 light nanoseconds.

It is noted, with some interest, that neither man nor dog was preyed upon by this vile creature, which is presumed to subsist purely on a diet of rabbits, fresh from the warren, which it is said to eat in great number.

...there is alwaies in his tracke or path left a glutinous and filmie matter (as by a smal similitude we may perceiue in a snailes)

Suggesting that perhaps it does indeed crawl upon its belly, like some kind of massive slug. Is what we have here a remnant of that ancient class of giant snail that was many-times painted in the borders of ancient books, rather than a dragon?

Magnitudo penarum, facit multitudo peccatorum, from the monsters of our sinnes, the monsters of our punishment increaseth.

Which means the dragon is kicking about and squirting folk with its icky goo, and eating all the bunnies, because the Sussexians are naughty people. I'm not sure I'd change my wicked ways because some guy had to run away from a giant slug in the forest somewhere. Just stay out of the bloody forest.

Interestingly, Iguanodon bones have been unearthed in the area around Sussex, so it's possible that dragonny tales come back to trying to explain these... though I suspect digging up a thigh-bone of an Iguanodon might make you think the 'dragon' was a smidge bigger than 9ft... but who knows?

Either way, Trundle's pamphlet had a wide audience, and was stored in various local libraries at the time. Only one remaining copy of the original is known to exist at the moment, in the Bodliean libraries: a group of 28 libraries that serve the University of Oxford.

Trundle himself was not really considered a byword for veracity, and his texts tended to be read with some skepticism. HIs works tended to be assessed as unreliable and exploitative... using shocking headlines to get readers involved and... well, essentially, preached to.

Hence the comments about the evils of man being the cause of the dragon, and one of the earliest forms of clickbait recorded.

Külmking of Estonia

This savage creature is a spirit which lives in the forests and swamps of Estonia. It feasts upon travelers, but especially upon those who disturb the natural world in which it lives.

Now, you might think "Oh... it's a forest protector, surely that's a good thing?" - and yes, under normal circumstances you might be right... but this particular forest protector eats children alive, and stalks nearby villages after dark.

It's not a 'Good Spirit with a Bad Rep'. It's a full-on savage paranormal horror. A ghost of an evil dead person.

You might think that's bad enough, but it gets even worse. This thing doesn't just kill and eat you, oh no. Though killing and eating its victims is most definitely on the playlist, Külmking's big party trick is to spirit-walk through people... turning mild mannered friendly individuals into evil shadows of their former selves. This way, it could rampage through an entire village, turning everyone into a serial killer.

It delights in turning good friends against each other in this manner... or wife against husband, or father against child. Külmking isn't just a villain...

Külmking is a total A-hole.

Sure, it protects the forest... and I'm all for protecting a forest... but you just can't come back from villainy of that magnitude. It would be like forgiving The Plague for wiping out one third of Europe because it once patted a kitten.

Külmking (which amusingly enough translates into English as "Cold Shoe") is one of those dark creatures that unscrupulous parents might tell their children will come and get them if they don't eat all their vegetables.

How did this villain meet its doom?

... it didn't. It's still out there, stalking the forests and swamps of Estonia to this day. (Cue the menacing music...)

Koschei The Deathless

Often described as an emaciated walking corpse - with skin so thin you can see his skeleton through it - Koschei (Russ: Кощéй) is fundamentally a villain who crops up in various tales as a foil or rival to the hero.

Why 'deathless'? Well, he has hidden his soul inside an egg, and hidden that egg inside an animal, and then hidden that animal inside a container... though tales vary. The upshot of this is that he cannot be killed, though I honestly wouldn't recommend you try this at home.

Koschei frequently appears to be benevolent to the story's hero at the outset. He will befriend, and then betray, anyone who dares to trust him. He has magic at his disposal, and is not beyond using it to take or gain advantage.

Now, maybe it's just me, but if he's described as a walking corpse, 'trust' would be a word so far down the list - notably, under 'fear' and 'suspicion' and 'running away very quickly' - that being betrayed by him would not really be an option.

He rides a seven legged horse (I can't even imagine this being remotely practical) and has magical artifacts to help him meet his nefarious goals.

How nefarious? Well, at one point Koschei hears of three beauties in a particular kingdom. He arrives there, promptly kills two, wounds the third, and for good measure petrifies (as stone) the entire kingdom, and abducts a princess.

As far as nefarious goes, that's right up there, I'm sure you'll agree.

However, as with most villains he ended badly. Russian heroic character Ivan Sosnovich (Russ: Иван Соснович) eventually tracks down his soul, smashes the egg, kills Koschei, and rescues the princess.

Which is nice and all, but I'm not sure where this leaves an entire petrified kingdom. In the safe-for-kiddies Grimm version, I'm sure they'd all have turned back to normal upon the villain's defeat... but some of these old tales can be pretty unforgiving.

So Koschei the Deathless simply became Koschei the Dead, and went on to have a fairly comprehensive career in movies and ballet... with his story being adapted several times over the years.

Lantern Men of the Fens

On those dark and misty nights when walking the fens of East Anglia, in England, don't try to bolster your worried spirits by whistling, lest you draw the attention and ire of a Lantern Man.

Ghostly apparitions of fearsome shape, a Lantern Man is an embodiment of malice. The tales tell of them attacking those who walk the fens[7]. They live in the reeds and the darkness, emit their own ghostly light, but will hunt down any who whistle, or cast light upon their domain.

With a guttural hiss, they will launch themselves from the reeds at anyone crossing the fens who has attracted their gaze and drag them into the marshes to drown.

The fens themselves are marshlands, ecologically diverse, and home to many myths and legends... and the lantern men - a sort of more pro-active will'o' the wisp - are among them.

In the 1870s, a man crossing the fens reported that he had whistled for his dog, and attracted the wrath of a Lantern Man. He was holding his own lamp but dropped it in fear as he ran. As he stopped to look behind him, the grotesque figure was kicking the lantern to bits, and hissing loudly. Naturally, he kept running, and lived to tell the tale.

Running is not the only way to avoid being murdered by a Lantern Man. If you lie face down with your mouth in the mud, they appear incapable of seeing you, and after stalking about for a while in anger, will drift back into the reeds, leaving you to stealthily make your escape.

As well as using physical force to attack their victims, a Lantern Man is said to be able to 'draw the breath from you', and can use fire (or heat, at least) to kill their victims.

Never whistle in the fens of East Anglia.

Lambton Worm

One Sunda morn young Lambton went a-fishing in the Wear;
An' catched a fish upon he's heuk he thowt leuk't vary queer.
But whatt'n a kind ov fish it was young Lambton cudden't tell.
He waddn't fash te carry'd hyem,so he hoyed it doon a well.[8]

Today, a tale of woe and worms. The Lambton worm, and poor John Lambton, who tested his luck a little too far by neglecting his church-going duties.

John Lambton was the heir of the Lambton Estate, County Durham in Northeast England, and he was not a particularly religious fellow. In the 1300s, however, some seven hundred (and change) years ago, to be without religion was to be really pushing your luck.

So, one Sunday when he should have been at church, John grabbed his fishing rod and made for a stream to fish for eels. On the way there, he met a strange old man who told him that the only thing he would catch would be misfortune and ruin, and that he should go to church, like a good little heir.

John didn't pay too much attention to the strange old man... which is where most of these tales start to go wrong.

Just for the sake of clarity, if you're doing something you probably shouldn't, and a strange old man pops out of nowhere and intones something dolorous at you... bloody-well do what you're told.

So, he begins to fish, but catches nothing but a small malformed worm of foul visage. With holes along the sides of its head, and fangs, and a foul slime. At first, he chucks it in his bucket, thinking to take it home... but he thinks back to the old man and, fearing he had caught something horrible, he flings it down a well.

Years pass, and John grows up. Feeling penitent for his rebellious youth, John joins the crusades, and heads to the Barbary Coast at the head of a great army. He is there for seven or more years, fighting fiercely.

While he's away, strange things start happening around the village. Livestock starts to go missing... at first only small things like chickens... then sheep... then cows... and then worryingly... people.

One day, a farmer sees a massive and ugly worm coiled around the base of a hill, finishing off the carcass of a cow. He barely escapes with his life but passes on the terrible tale to John's aged father, the Lord of Lambton.

At first, the Lord sends a few of his men to dispatch the creature, but they are eaten without too much trouble... and the fearsome beast follows their riderless horses home to Lambton Castle, where it goes on a reign of terror, uprooting trees, smashing homes and people, and generally getting underfoot.

Lord Lambton manages to subdue it with the milk of nine good cows... something which must be repeated daily, lest the creature consume everyone and everything for miles around.

Periodically, knights will try their courage and steel on the beast... which would, without fail, kill and devour them. Even if they cut chunks off the worm, they grow back together again into one disgusting wormy whole.

At this point I'd be thinking "How much arsenic can you lay your hands on?" and "How much would it take to poison a worm that could wind itself three times around the castle?" - and then I figure they probably thought of this, and it didn't work. Typical.

John eventually returns from the Crusades and finds his land destitute. So much has been spent placating the worm that the entire region is falling into ruin... so John vows to kill the creature... especially since the strange old man turns up again and tells him that the whole thing is his fault, and this was the same worm he lobbed down the well.

The thing that annoys me about strange old folk who pop up to give warnings is that they're never particularly specific. If the old guy had said "If you catch a worm, hit it in the head with a brick, and then mulch it", rather than "your path leads to a tale of woe", then this whole messy situation could have been avoided.

The old fellow gives him some advice and tells him how to kill the worm... to cover his armour in spear heads before he attacks it... but warns that in order to avoid a crippling death-curse, he must also kill the first living thing he sees after he's killed the worm. This sort of thing never ends well.

So, now looking like a plate-metal hedgehog, John rides out to attack the beast. It curls itself around him and squeezes... and the spear heads penetrate its slippery body. In defence, it squeezes harder, causing the spear heads to rip even further into the beast.

All this time, John is laying about him with his might sword, cleaving off pieces of worm which - unfortunately, grow back into the beast... but it cannot drive out the spikes. The more it squeezes or struggles, the more damage it will do.

John leads the fight to the river, and again starts lopping chunks off the creature. The fast river water carries the pieces away before they can re-attach, and eventually the creature is just a head, which eventually dies.

Now, John must kill the first thing he sees... so he had arranged with his father to release a dog, which would run to him. Alas, his idiot father forgot, and ran in himself. John cannot bring himself to kill his father, so declares the job done.

Alas, the creature's curse is quite specific, and from this point on, every male heir to the Lambton line will die young, and in violence, rather than peacefully of old age.

The tale of the Lambton Worm was heavily referenced in Bram Stoker's "Lair of the White Worm", which itself became a somewhat successful niche 80's indy movie starring Hugh Grant, Peter Capaldi, and Amanda Donohoe.

Notably, while the tale itself is just a tale, the Lambton family, and the Lambton estate and castle are real.

Lady of Shalott and Personal Isolation

Apropos of nothing... I'm not a soppy lad by nature. If you gave me the choice between a villainous dragon or a sad lady staring wistfully out of a tower window, I would normally be trying to cajole the dragon into giving me a free ride so we could throw stones at the tower.

The Lady of Shalott, however, is a tale of sadness and isolation all tied into Arthurian legend, and as such, I have a sort-of genetic predisposition towards sympathy. One is Welsh, after all. Also, this was written at the height of the pandemic, so "not getting out much" was a bit of a theme.

Based on the 13th century tale of *Elaine of Astolat* (*Demoiselle d'Escalot*), this legend has been adapted many times, including probably the most famous telling by *Alfred, Lord Tennyson* in the first half of the 19th century.

And by the moon the reaper weary,
Piling sheaves in uplands airy,
Listening, whispers, "'Tis the fairy
Lady of Shalott."

The lady suffers from a mysterious curse which prevents her from gazing upon the world outside her island tower, so she gazes upon a mirror and weaves what she sees instead. Through his verse, Tennyson explores the relationship between artistry and personal isolation - something which is perhaps familiar to more than a few given the current state of the world.

The Lady of Shalott is desperately lonely and forced to experience the outside world only through the mirror, and her ephemeral web of woven reminiscences. The sad result for The Lady is that when she finally sees something in the world which is, in her mind, worth looking at (Lancelot - Knight of the Round Table, and friend of King Arthur), she looks directly at him - with disastrous consequences.

Out flew the web and floated wide—
The mirror crack'd from side to side;
"The curse is come upon me," cried
The Lady of Shalott.

She finds a boat, writes her name upon it, and drifts down the river towards Camelot to meet Lancelot. Alas, she dies before reaching the shore. One of the people who sees her as the boat beaches itself is Lancelot, who thinks she is lovely.

I have certain opinions about Lancelot which are

probably shared by more than a few. He's a bit of a cad and a bounder in my book. Tennyson's work suggests he turned the head of more than one fair lady. Perhaps he should be the villain of this tale - though his role is perhaps too passive in this case.

Can, I hear you ask, Personal Isolation really be described as villainous? Yes, I am aware that I am stretching the definition of Villainy near to breaking point, but I think so. It is an issue faced by many at the moment, and the potential social ramifications really shouldn't be ignored. It's more nebulous than a cad or a bounder and doesn't have the same on-screen appeal as a villainous dragon... but still.

Indulge me. I've managed to get myself hooked on folk music recently, and I've gone all introspective. I'll get over it and be listening to thrash metal again in no time. My favourite version of Shalott in song is written by folk-singer Deborah Rose, and I urge you to look her up online.

Loch Ness Monster

In the wilds of Scotland, where no man dares to tread is a loch - Loch Ness: A sort of long lake, except a bit more tartan - and in that loch there lives a mythical creature that has defied description. So, I won't try.

THE EARLY DAYS

The recorded first sighting of a creature in the loch is in the sixth century AD, when a monk reported a man being buried beside Loch Ness. Those burying him explained he had been mauled by a horrific aquatic creature while swimming in the loch.

There's not a lot that - for want of a better term - legitimately lives in Scottish lochs, apart from the occasional eel, some minnows, teeny little lampreys and such... so chances are that it wasn't anything normal that killed this poor fellow.

My money is on a mugging gone bad. When you're burying the evidence, and a monk turns up I could see a hastily contrived conversation:

Monk: What's going on here, lads?
Person1: Uh... where did you come fr... uh... well, Dave was swimming, and something stabbed...
Person2: Bit, Mike, Bit!
Person1: Uh, yeah... bit. Something bit him,

and we tried to rescue him, but it kept stabbing...

Person2: Biting!

Person1: Yeah... Biting him until he handed over the... I mean, until he died. So, we're like, burying him here before the rozzers...

Person2: Crows! Vultures!

Person1: ... um... find him?

This feels a lot more believable to me than a monster... but it was over a thousand years ago, so who really knows what was going on then, right?

The monk then decided to get one of his followers to swim across the loch - which is a dick-move at best - and as this poor gullible idiot made off from the shore, a creature approached him.

The monk supposedly made the sign of the cross and called out "Go no further. Do not touch the man. Go back at once!", and the creature vanished below the waves.

I'm sceptical... but the monk was eventually sainted, and I'm sure his reported banishment of the supposed monster had more than a little something to do with it.

He probably had at least a couple of 'witnesses' who were more than happy to back up his version of events, rather than have someone explore alternatives.

Also, some tales point to this occurring in the River

Ness, rather than the Loch Ness... so what's more likely? A Loch monster or a River monster? (Shrug)

MORE RECENT SIGHTINGS

There was a long hiatus of recorded sightings until things kicked off again in the 1800s.

- D. McKenzie (1871) - saw a large wriggling creature in the water
- Macdonald (1888) - saw a stubbly legged creature swim from the shore
- G. Spicer (1933) - saw the creature cross the road in front of his car and enter the water
- H. Gray (1933) - took a famous photograph of the creature in the water
- Grant (1934) - nearly ran it over on his motorbike
- R. Wilson (1934) - took the famous photograph of the long necked something

There were certainly plenty of others, but the point is that none of the sightings was able to present any kind of useful evidence that couldn't easily be explained some other way, and some were even able to be proven to be fraudulent.

Either way, the Loch Ness Monster is firmly entrenched in pop-culture now, and millions of pounds have been (and still are) spent combing the waters for any kind of evidence of its existence.

The creature forms a notable portion of tourist income for the region, and it's definitely in the interest of the locals to keep the legends alive... so it's no surprise to me that the occasional sighting still occurs.

Heck, the creature even supposedly appears on Apple Maps satellite imagery of the loch as a large whale-like creature some 100ft long.

Though Apple Maps also famously showed an English train station in the middle of a field, and totally missed the fact that Stratford-Upon-Avon (where Shakespeare was born) even existed, and for some reason decided an entire sheep farm was a major international airport... so I'm not entirely sure how valuable such sightings are. Later analysis suggests it's a boat wake, anyway.

There have been plenty of explanations as to what the Scottish Monster might be, if there is any physicality to the sightings. From otters seen through mist, to elephants swimming in the water (Seriously. Because Scotland and elephants. You know that whole link there), to floating tree trunks, and even a Greenland Shark.

A Greenland Shark might even explain an attack. These things can get up to 20ft long, can survive in fresh water, and there would be enough for them to eat in the loch, which does connect to the ocean. (Albeit in a slightly round-about way)

... and let's not forget hoaxes. Because people will be people.

In short, it's a fun tale, and it would be amazing if there was any kind of truth to it, but we live in a technological environment where anything as big as this creature is supposed to be would have been found by now - given several sonar, visual, and DNA scans of the loch and its surrounds.

Loup-Garou

There are vampire tales, and werewolf tales, and even tales where vampires and werewolves coexist and either fight each other or work together... and then there's Louisiana, where you get both in one body, and you won't like it one little bit.

The fog hangs low on the top of the bayou. You can see it to the back, you can see it to the fro. It hangs o'er your shoulder like the mists are getting bolder, and the red eyes glow.

You may hear a howl. You may hear a scurry of worryingly heavy footfalls... but it's the hot breath on the back of your neck that prompts you to turn around slowly.

Never turn around slowly. If you find yourself suddenly living out a horror movie, you should just run. If something is breathing down the back of your neck in the middle of a bayou, and you're not there with your bestest girl, you best be making rooster-tails across the swamp, with how fast you be running.

Because it might be the Loup-Garou.

If you were to describe a Lou-Garou, it's basically a werewolf. An anthropomorphised wolf in semi-human form, with an insatiable appetite for blood.

What happens is that someone is cursed by a witch or, more frequently, just became one due to some bad management, such as failing to confess your sins during Easter. Which seems extreme.

A Loup-Garou will stalk the Louisiana swamps - the punishment mostly being that you have to live in the swamp and live off whatever you can find in there during the night... but in daytime you return to your human form.

Just eat during the day, and when you're half-dog just hang out in your room and sleep all the bloody time like my dog did. I guess the whole point of inflicting lycanthrope on someone though is that it's supposed to be inconvenient. Not "a great way to have a rest of an evening".

It's not a permanent curse... you're stuck with it for 101 days... a little over three months... but you don't just get better. You have to bite someone else to pass on the curse.

That person is then the Loup-Garou for 101 days, and you go back to being a normal person... and presumably you're no longer flexible enough to lick your own bottom.

You can also break the curse if someone recognises you in wolf form and manages to draw some blood from you. Presumably you'd be trying to eat their face through this whole incident, so chances are nobody's going to be going out of their way to lend a hand.

It gets more awkward than that, however, because once the curse is broken, neither you, nor the person who helped break the curse, can ever say anything about it, otherwise an even worse fate will befall them.

It's undefined what this worse fate will be, but it's presumably something to do with turning into stuff... or maybe a sudden appreciation for Nickelback or Creed.

If someone were to draw some blood from you, and you reverted to human form, and you were both standing there in the swamp looking awkwardly at each other, and one of you was naked and had no idea how they'd got there... chances are you'd probably mutually decide to never talk about it anyway.

Anyway... Loup-Garou... becoming a sort of lend/lease-lycanthrope because you were a bad Catholic. The loup-garou stories tend to be warning tales, rather than violent tales. Cajun werewolves have a tendency to terrify rather than tear-apart.

Mordiford Dragon

It's all very well having your child bring home a kitten or a puppy found wandering in the neighbourhood and asking if they can keep it... but what happens if they bring home a baby dragon?

Mordiford is a village in Herefordshire, in the West Midlands of England. It's a picturesque little place, spanning a natural and ancient ford over the river Lugg.

Maud was a young girl who used to live in Mordiford. It is not clear in the tales precisely when, but likely to be some time around the early to mid-1700s.

One day while out exploring the land around the village, she came across a curious creature. A cute and tiny little lizard, with wings. She immediately snatched it up and took it home to show her parents.

They recognised it as a wyvern - one of the lesser dragons - and insisted that she return it to where it came from, so that it would go about its way, and not cause problems for the village. Maud pretended to do so, but in-fact kept the creature in a nearby barn and fed it daily on milk to keep it calm.

As the story goes, the creature grew quickly, and

eventually became too big to hide, so Maud took it back to the forest in which she found it and found a safe place for it to live. She would return to the forest daily to play with her friend, and watch it learn to fly.

The problem with wyvern is that they're not precisely friendly. They're notorious man-eaters, and sure enough, as the creature became larger, milk wasn't enough to assuage its growing hunger.

At first it began to target sheep and cows, and then when the farmers tried to stop it, it started to attack people from the village... finding human flesh delicious.

Maud tried to reason with the creature but, while it would not harm her, everybody else seems to have been fair game. It may have been a small dragon, but it was still a dragon, after all.

Eventually, the villagers petitioned the nobles of Mordiford, who sent a knight, in full armour, to rid the land of this dangerous creature. The knight, Garston, hunted the creature in the forest, and eventually found its lair, where he deflected a blast of liquid fire with his shield, and smote the creature with his lance, killing it where it stood.

Maud burst from the forest to mourn her pet... but the village of Mordiford was now safe from the fell beast.

In some tales, the creature lived until as late as

1811, and a mural was even painted on the wall of the Mordiford church... though the vicar ordered it removed, because dragons were considered a sign of the devil.

These days Mordiford has a dragon trail, and tourists can wander the area around the village, and see the places in which the tale supposedly took place.

Mordiford Dragon

"Maud took it back to the forest in which she found it and found a safe place for it to live."

Mahaha

Up in the Arctic North, where the snows have many names, and burn as fiercely as the fires in the south, the Inuit people have lived for generations. With them was born a particular set of survival skills, and a depth of mythology which many others might find quite strange.

Let's talk about Mahaha. A tall humanoid creature, looking so thin as to be almost emaciated. This demonic fiend has pale blue skin, is as cold as ice to the touch, and has bright white eyes that peek through stringy white hair.

The creature's hands are large, with long fingers, and at the end of each finger, a hideous gnarled talon, blue as if painted, and sharper than the tooth of any shark.

Mahaha is a demon of the ice wastes, and does not fear the cold. It can appear as if from nowhere, unclothed and grinning from ear to ear with an expression so predatory that even the hardiest of hunters could faint well away.

I can see you thinking "Well, there are plenty of mythological creatures that will tear you limb from limb with their awful claws, and probably eat you thereafter." - but Mahaha is somewhat less usual in that regard.

You see, when someone freezes to death, their lips can contract in a rictus grin, as if they died smiling. The legend therefore goes that Mahaha would tickle his victims to death with his terrifying claws.

Nobody - when attacked by this demon - could stop themselves from laughing to death, and then, when they are dead and their soul consumed by the demon, their body would be left in the snow for others to find.

Not all is lost, however. Most of the tales that involve Mahaha give an idea as to how to defeat the beast. If you're lucky enough to have opened a waterhole through the ice, or can convince the demon to wait until you have one - invite it to drink of the waters.

When the beast leans down to drink from the open waterhole, give it a swift kick in the pants (assuming it is wearing any), and the beast will fall into the water. Mahaha cannot swim, and plummets like a stone into the depths.

Not many demonic creatures would be kind enough to wait for you to dig a hole through the ice, but Mahaha apparently is... so remember this, and should you be approached by an ugly naked skinny guy in the arctic wastes... remember this tale. Your life may depend upon it.

Mares of Diomedes

Greek mythology is full of unpleasantness. Monsters and villains abound, and if you were never a fan of horses to begin with, you might be horrified to find out about the man-eating Mares of Diomedes, also known as the Mares of Thrace.

Diomedes was the King of Thrace, in the north-east of Greece, covering what is now parts of Greece and Bulgaria.[9]

The hero Heracles (greatest of the Hellenic chthonic heroes) was sent by King Eurystheus (these guys sound like skin diseases) of Tiryns to steal the mares from Diomedes. Essentially posh horse rustling... and a bit more dangerous, because the creatures were always mad with hunger, and quite keen to eat anyone who got too close to them.

Now, for some reason Eurystheus neglected to tell Heracles that the horses were man-eaters. I suppose if you wanted someone to nick something for you, you might skimp on some of the details... but that seems like a bit of a doozy.

Anyway, because Heracles figured they were just nice horses, after he stole them, he left them in the care of a young lad called Abderus so that he could pop back up the hill and fight Diomedes himself.

Naturally, the mares - being a bit peckish at this point - ate the boy. Heracles was... well, to say he was pissed would be putting it mildly. He was so angry, that he took the defeated Diomedes, and fed him to his own horses.

Eating people apparently calms the horses down for a bit, so Heracles was able to quickly take the horses back to King Eurystheus without further incident... upon which they became permanently docile and were allowed to wander the isle of Argos by themselves.

Frankly, I'm surprised that Heracles didn't get a bit more grumpy at Eurystheus for leaving out vital information which might have helped to avoid Abderus (and Diomedes) getting eaten... but this seems to have been glossed over somewhat in the prose.

Either way... after having brought back the (once) man-eating mares, Eurystheus sent Heracles off to steal the Girdle of Hippolyta. Probably neglecting to mention the fact that it explodes or something.

Heracles and Hercules are basically the same person - one from a Greek perspective and one from a Roman. The theft of the mares was the eighth of his 12 Labours from popular mythology.

Māui

Māui forms the basis of many Māori and Polynesian legends. He is a demigod of supernatural parents with a penchant for cleverness, curiosity, and trickery.

He has a bit of a reputation for using ancestor's jawbones for weapons, fishhooks, and so forth, and is a bit slapdash when it comes to satisfying his curiosity.

This is the tale of how Māui brought fire to the Māori people.

Technically speaking, the Māori people already had fire. They carefully nurtured their campfires, always ensuring that at least one was always burning. The fire could be spread from one to the other, so they were never without.

This is the bit where I suspect Māui has the hallmarks of villainy. Tricksters often are at least a little villainous.

Māui was relaxing near one of the fires one evening, and his curiosity piqued. "Where does fire come from?", he wondered.

Rather than... you know... ask someone, he waited until everyone was asleep, and ran around all of the campfires in all of the land and extinguished them all.

When the people awoke the following day, there was no fire, and they were extremely worried.

How shall we cook our food? How will we keep warm at night? How can we live without fire?

The people asked their Rangatira (chief) - who also happened to be Māui's father. He thought long and hard and said "The great goddess Mahuika is the keeper of fire. Someone must go to her and ask for some."

Māui was pleased that his trickery was working, so he volunteered to go. The Rangatira warned him, "You may be a demigod, but you must show respect to the great goddess. Mahuika will not take kindly to trickery or deceit!"

Māui basically shrugged this off and skipped off to the fire mountain in which Mahuika lived. He found a dark cave at the base of the mountain and crept in.

There, in all her fiery glory was Mahuika - wreathed in flame, but eyeless. She sniffed as Māui entered, and in a voice that shook the very foundations of the Earth asked, "Who approaches Mahuika?"

Māui replied, "I am Māui-tikitiki-a-Taranga, and all of the fires in the world have been extinguished. I come to respectfully ask for more, so that we may cook our food and warm our homes."

Mahuika was impressed by Māui's respectful nature, so she pulled off one of her fiery fingernails and gave it to him, bidding him return to the people with the gift of fire.

Māui took the burning fingernail and made his way back.

However, being even more curious about the origins of fire, he wondered what might happen if there were no fire left in the world and Mahuika had none to give... so her threw the fingernail into a river, extinguishing it, and ran back to the cave.

"Apologies, great goddess Mahuika! I accidentally dropped the fingernail into the river. May I have another?"

Mahuika seemed to like Māui, so she pulled off another flaming fingernail, and gave it to him.

Māui threw this one into the river as well, and came back again,

"Alas - a fish splashed the nail as I was crossing the river, may I have one more?"

This went on for a little while, until Mahuika was down to only one fingernail, and she was very cross. She hurled the nail at Māui, attempting to burn him to death, but Māui changed himself into a bird and flew high into the air.

The fire followed him, but ultimately fell back to Earth, and set fire to everything. The whole world started to burn, and Māui was panicking. Desperately, he called upon his ancestor

Tāwhirimātea (God of the winds) for help.

Tāwhirimātea atua o ngā hau e whā, āwhinatia mai!

A great wind sprang up, and water was whipped up into thick clouds, which fell upon the land - dousing the mountain of fire and diminishing Mahuika's power greatly.

The fire which had burned across the land fled from the waters and hid inside the wood of the Tōtara and Kaikōmako trees.

Māui returned to the people but was not bearing fire. They were angry with him, until he showed them the wood that he had brought.

Swiftly rubbing together Tōtara sticks, Māui watched with glee as the fire sprang out. He caught it, and put it into the bonfire, and the Māori people once more had fire, and a means to produce it forever without having to beg for it from the gods.

Mictlāntēcutli

Lots of civilisations had a god of the dead, and the Aztecs were no exception. Theirs was particularly perilous, and the worship of this deity would sometimes involve ritual cannibalism.

When you hear about Aztecs in various media these days, it tends to be horrifying tales of ritual sacrifice... and those tales are certainly embellished, but not by as much as you might think.

Mictlāntēcutli was one of the higher-up deities on the Aztec totem-pole, and lived in one of the lower parts of their underworld. He was often depicted wearing human bones, with a skull-like face, and a flamboyant headdress.

The stars would descend into his open jaw as they descended at the end of each night, and he would stand with his arms raised, as he was poised to tear apart the dead who would enter the demesne surrounding his underworld home.

Associations and the Calendar

Mictlāntēcutli is associated with several types of animal... such as owls, spiders, bats... and is fifth in influence of the nine gods of the night.

I'm not even going to try to explain the Aztec

calendar... there's another article all by itself... but Mictlāntēcutli was one of the 20 deities associated with the calendar, and all people born on the sixth day of their 13 day week were said to have souls that sprang from him.

Of those 13 weeks, Mictlāntēcutli was the sort-of backup god for the tenth week of their 20 week cycle, in-case that other god had other things to do, presumably.

The Birth of Mankind

In the mythology of the Aztec, Mictlāntēcutli was also the guardian of the bones of dead gods. When the younger gods Quetzalcoatl and Xolotl were sent to steal the bones of the previous generation of gods, so that they could make new gods, it was Mictlāntēcutli who blocked their path.

Quetzalcoatl managed to gather up the bones, but Mictlāntēcutli attacked him, and Quetzalcoatl dropped them. The bones shattered into myriad pieces, unable to be put back together.

There's a fairly complex sub-tale here involving Quetzalcoatl using a shell to make trumpet noises, and bees, and a time limit, and worms, and... well... long story short..

Distracting Mictlāntēcutli, Quetzalcoatl managed to flee the underworld with the damaged shards -

and from them, the gods were able to create many of the mortal creatures that populate the world today, including mankind.

The villainy presumably being that if Mictlāntēcutli hadn't caused all the bones to be shattered, then mankind would have been a race of pure immortals, rather than the mud-grubbing short-lives that we apparently are.

Grave Goods

If you died in Aztec times, you were buried with a variety of grave-goods, to ease your passage into the underworld. The higher quality the items with which you were buried, the better you would fare in the afterlife.

This is a fairly universal thing across many religions... but in Aztec culture, the dead would gift the items with which they were buried to Mictlāntēcutli and his wife... and good luck to you if they were deemed not good enough... because there are no second chances in the afterlife.

Let's face it... if you're described as a "God of the Dead", you're never going to be considered a heroic character in any mythology.

Mictlāntēcutli

"When the younger gods were sent to steal the bones of the previous generation of gods, so that they could make new gods, it was Mictlāntēcutli who blocked their path."

Nebraska Salt Hag

An old tale from Nebraska in which a native American chief encounters something unusual, and a new custom is born.

The Platte River flows across the Nebraska plains, and where it meets the bitter waters of the Saline River, there was a native American tribe eking out a living from the rough terrain.

They were a warlike people, and the chief himself was prone to rage, which caused no end of trouble with the tribe's relationships with others who lived nearby.

I can find no reference to any particular tribal group, as all the versions of the tale I have seen have excluded this detail. A good many tribes are linked to Nebraska, including (but not limited to) Cheyenne, Comanche, Dakota, Kiowa, and Pawnee.

The chief was strong-willed and a brutal warrior, but his wife - whom he loved dearly - could tame his wild rages, and together they both ruled well, and the people began to prosper.

They lacked for little, except for the salt to keep them healthy under the deadly Nebraska sun. This was in short supply, and hard to find.

Alas, misfortune struck in the shape of a concealed snake, and the chief's wife died. Locked into mourning, the chief hid himself away in his lodge, and would be seen by no one.

This went on for a long time, and there were rumbles among the tribe about replacing him with one of the younger, more level-headed warriors.

Hearing these rumblings blown by the wind through the gaps in his lodge walls, the chief decided to take action. He dressed himself in his war clothes, and strode out of his lodge and west, into the desert.

After travelling far, the chief was exhausted, and threw himself down to sleep on the ground. He felt he had only just closed his eyes when he heard screaming.

Standing instantly, and battle-ready, the chief saw two figures fighting, both women. One was a furious old hag who - twisted in visage, and clearly evil - despite her age, seemed spry and incredibly strong. She was attacking a younger woman with her tomahawk, and it looked as if she was about to win and claim herself a scalp.

In shock, the chief recognised the younger woman as his wife - though how this was possible, he did not know - and he leapt into battle to save her.

He fought the old crone to a standstill, both of them standing exhausted, but neither willing to concede defeat. After a few short moments to catch their breath the fighting resumed, and the hag - who due to her strength and fury was clearly a supernatural creature - looked as if she was about to win.

With supreme effort, the chief dodged her last attack and buried his own hatchet into the wicked woman's brain. Before she died, she leapt, grasped the chief's wife by the hair, and with one last smug look back at him over her shoulder, the earth opened and swallowed them both as the chief leapt forward, crying out in a combination of loss, and horror, and anger.

Moments later, the earth rumbled, and a massive pillar of salt tore up out of the ground where the hag and the chief's wife had vanished.

The chief - now much improved from his previous torpor - returned to the village and told everyone what he had seen. Salt was an important commodity under the hot Nebraska sun, so the tribe travelled to see the sight.

For many years, they gathered salt there, but knowing that the huge pillar was under the protection of the being they came to label the 'salt witch', they would beat the ground around it with clubs and hatchets, believing that each blow would be felt by the evil creature, and stop her from emerging to hurt anyone else.

The chief remained the chief of the tribe, but he would frequently set out into the Nebraska wilds for a month at a time, searching for his stolen wife.

Nuckelavee

*Of the coast of Northern Scotland you'll find Orkney...
an archipelago famous for containing some of the
oldest neolithic sites in Europe, no trees, gorgeous
white sandy beaches, dramatic cliffs, and a lot of wind
and rain. It's also home to a bizarre skinless centaur
who you definitely don't want to meet.*

Orkney doesn't really have a shortage of
supernatural critters, but there's little that used
to generate as much fear and trepidation as
Nukelavee. This beast was evil, and his one pleasure
(and one would argue, hobby) was tormenting the
islanders.

Some would call him a centaur. Others would claim
he was a vile melding of horse and rider. A complete
horse (albeit cyclopean) and the upper torse of a
man sticking out of its back, almost as if riding it,
but an actual body part, with muscles and blood
and sinews shared.

The human head was far too large, with a wide
mouth - almost a snout - and a single bright red
eye that glowed in the low light like an ember on a
dying fire.

Without skin, the creature was in entirety an open
wound of raw flesh, with visibly pulsing veins and

arteries full of thick black blood. The arms on the human part of him could reach to the ground, giving it, in effect, six legs.

The creature's breath was said to be so foul that it would blight anyone who smelled it, and it would use this as a weapon - dropping those who would confront it with foul diseases.

Given Orkney's heavily Norse influenced heritage, it should come as no surprise that the origins of the Nuckelavee character are also Norse. Surprisingly for a creature described as mostly horse, it is primarily a sea-dweller.

Orkney was a difficult place to eke out a living back in the pre-modern era, and if there was a drought, then it was Nuckelavee's work. Ditto and blight or disease upon the crops, or sickness that spread through the population... all wrought by this foul creature or its breath.

You would think that this foul and seemingly undefeatable creature would have driven all life off Orkney, but for two facts:

1. That during the summer months, Nuckelavee was restrained by the Mither o' the Sea, an ancient spirit which lived in the ocean, and did what it could for the islanders.
2. That it could not stand fresh water... and given that it could certainly rain in

Orkney, this tended to keep the beast hidden in its lair - in the waters just off-shore - unless it was driven into a rage.

For the same reason, you could - if you were fast enough - escape it by running through a stream, for Nuckelavee could not cross unless it could find a narrow enough place to jump across, or stones upon which to stand.

So... what would drive it into a rage?

There was a practice on Orkney of fertilising fields with kelp, gathered from the shoreline and burned upon a bonfire. This burning produced a nutrient rich ash, which when spread upon the fields would help to produce great crops in the otherwise poor soil.

Nuckelavee did not like this practice, and crop burning would send him into an absolute frenzy, spewing disease and death across the islands - at one point wiping out all of the horses in one island, and afflicting people in another.

As with most malevolent myths from bygone eras, Nuckelavee likely acts as a proxy for explaining the diseases that would have run rampant through island communities - the people, the crops, and the animals... but the tales remain, nevertheless.

Perseus as Villain

In Greek mythology Perseus is a heroic demigod figure who killed monsters and founded Mycenae. He is portrayed as the hero in popular fiction - notably Clash of the Titans (1981 & 2010) and is perhaps best known for beheading Medusa in order to save Andromeda from the Kraken. (Though, it was the sea-monster Cetus in the myth.)

So... why do I think he was a villain rather than a hero?

You only have to look at the Medusa story to get some insight in that regard.

Medusa was a monster, to be sure. She had snakes for hair and could turn people to stone if they looked into her eyes. However, the name Medusa means 'guardian' or 'she who protects'.

The Roman poet Ovid regales us with his story of Medusa as an incredibly beautiful woman. So beautiful, that she had suitors coming from all over the known world to court her. She was raped by Poseidon in Athena's temple.

The Greek gods being somewhat mercurial, Athena (who had a bit of a thing for Poseidon) got a bit pissy about this whole incident and cursed her. The curse stripped Medusa of her beauty, transformed her hair to serpents, and made it so that whoever gazed into her eyes would turn to stone.

Perseus States:

She was once most beautiful, and the jealous aspiration of many suitors. Of all her beauties none was more admired than her hair: I came across a man who recalled having seen her. They say that Neptune (Poseidon), lord of the seas, violated her in the temple of Minerva (Athena). Jupiter's (Zeus's) daughter turned away, and hid her chaste eyes behind her aegis. So that it might not go unpunished, she changed the Gorgon's hair to foul snakes.
- Ovid's Metamorphoses (Kline) Book 4 [753-803]

Perseus - in Ovid's tale - thought this was perfectly reasonable a punishment from the Gods.

So, in the early tales, he does not seek Medusa's head to save Andromeda... he seeks her head because King Polydectes of Seriphus asked him to, because the King wants to marry his mother.

At this point, Medusa is in the company of her two sisters, who have vowed to protect her from all harm in the wake of her vile treatment by the Gods.

Perseus sneaks in while all three of the sisters are asleep, kills the sleeping Medusa (with the help of weapons provided by the Gods) and beheads her. Turns out she's pregnant with Poseidon's baby at the time - but that didn't seem to faze Perseus.

As her head comes off, the flying horse Pegasus springs from her body.

As an aside, later, a good buddy of Perseus called Bellerophon captures Pegasus and rides him into battle.

So, I'm inclined to think that it's not so much Medusa who was the villain of the early Greek tales. Sure, she was a monster who could turn you to stone with a glance, but it doesn't really sound like it was her fault.

I might be inclined to think that the Greek Gods were the villains, if it wasn't for the fact that I don't want to find myself riding the lightning... just on the off chance, y'know?

So, Perseus... the guy who killed the innocent pregnant victim of the Gods because his soon-to-be father-in-law wanted him to? He's the baddie in this one. Don't believe everything you see in the movies.

Perseus

"Perseus sneaks in while all three of the sisters are asleep, kills the sleeping Medusa and beheads her."

Penhill Giant

Settle in, for this is likely to be a long one, replete with terror, craziness, and woe. Grab a blanket, lower the lights, listen to the rain on the roof as the fire crackles in the hearth, and the cat purrs on your lap.

Penhill is in Wensleydale, Yorkshire, in the north of England. It was a lovely place back in the day, over a thousand years ago, before the Normans invaded. A farming community, and a quiet, idyllic spot, were it not for the giant. His tale is ancient.

Descended from Thor, and brought over by the Norse invaders, the Giant had built himself a large fortress on Penhill Beacon. There he lived with his faithful boarhound called Wolfhead, and one terrified servant. All around was his massive flock of pigs.

The Giant was cruel and much feared by the villagers. Occasionally, if they met on the roads or fields, the giant would throw boulders at them; careless as to whether they lived or died.

One day, a farmer's wall fell during a storm, and his sheep escaped up onto the beacon. The following morning, as the farmer's daughter, Gunda, was trying to round them up, the giant came across them as he was tending his own flock of pigs.

Laughing, he ordered Wolfhead to attack the sheep, and the enormous dog began to tear them apart, one at a time, terrifying the flock and scattering them.

Gunda ran up to the giant, and on her knees appealed to him to please stop killing the sheep, for they were all that stood between her family and starvation. The giant laughed and set his dog on her.

The brave shepherdess picked up a stone, and belted the attacking Wolfhead on the nose, sending him whimpering back to its master who, in a fit of rage, raised his club and killed the poor girl outright.

He then returned to his castle, not at all ashamed of the evil he had wrought and went to sleep.

The following morning, Wolfhead - who had been out scanning the flock - came back to report that one of the pigs had gone missing.

Enraged, the giant kicked the boarhound across the room, and screamed at it "You lazy hound! Go and find the missing pig, and then take me to it!"

Hurt, and confused, the loyal beast limped from the castle, and ran around the beacon until he found the pig. Dead. Upon investigating, the giant found a hunting arrow lodged in the pig's heart.

Angered, he turned to return to the castle, but

Wolfhead had become afraid of the giant, and refused to go with him. The boarhound instead bolted for the forest... but chased down by the giant, he was soon captured, and the giant swung his mighty club and killed his only friend.

Returning to the castle alone, the giant kicked his servant, and ordered him to go down to the village, and bring every male who could carry a bow. Any who refused to come would be killed, and their families along with them.

The servant, battered and bruised, did as he was told, and before long dozens of villagers were gathered in the giant's courtyard. Surly, with an undercurrent of anger which the giant had not seen before in this previously cowed group of people.

"Tell me!" the giant intoned "which among you killed my pig!"

The men looked around at each other, but no answer was forthcoming. "TELL ME!" the giant thundered and raised his club as if to kill them all.

"My lord, they do not know!" his servant called out, a cry that likely saved the men's lives, but further angered the giant. He back-handed the servant across the room, where the poor man lay dazed.

"If you will not tell me", the giant growled "then you will learn just how much I value my flock. Tomorrow morning, you will all return, and bring with you your oldest child."

From the back, a mysteriously robed old man called out "And what will you do, when they are still unable to give you an answer?"

The giant merely grinned with malice and shot back "Then they shall learn what I am capable of doing."

The old man leaned forward on his staff, his voice ringing clear across the courtyard. "Tomorrow is Thor's Day, and I tell you this... if one drop of blood is spilled on your lands, you will not enter your castle again, be you dead or alive!"

Outraged by the man's forwardness, but too shocked to take immediate action, the giant merely sputtered and gaped as the villagers left the castle and began the walk back to the village. He vowed, however, that his will would be enforced.

Ignoring his injured servant, the giant angrily tore apart and ate one of his pigs, in front of the large fireplace in his main hall.

The following morning when he awoke, he strode out into the courtyard as the sun was rising. He could see the men approaching up the beacon in the distance... but before him were nine slaughtered pigs, each with arrows through their hearts.

Enraged, the giant screamed for his servant, and demanded answers. When the poor man was unable provide any, the giant punched him practically through the courtyard wall, and left him for dead.

The poor servant, broken and bleeding almost beyond hope, found the reserves of strength to stand and slowly limp back to the great hall, where the fire still smouldered from the night before. Here, he began to pull curtains and banners and rugs and furs from the walls and floor and pile them onto the embers.

The giant exited the castle, and immediately outside the gates he found nine more slaughtered pigs, and nine more a few steps down the road. Looking about, he saw dozens of dead pigs, each with a single arrow through its heart.

Enraged, he screamed "By the great Thor, I will kill you all, and the beacon shall run red with the blood of your children! Then I shall descend to the village, and butcher all your families, and flocks, as my own flock has been butchered!"

But the men of Penhill had been brutalised enough. They had not brought their children, they had brought their bows, and they stood there angry, and knowing that even together they likely stood no chance against the incandescent giant.

With a roar of defiance from both sides, it seemed that battle was about to commence, when the mysterious old man appeared between them, almost as if by magic.

Calmly, he turned to the giant, and said "Can you

not see by your own actions that you are already undone? Afore these men even climbed the beacon, you had doomed yourself, for you have spilled blood on Thor's day, and he has renounced you."

The giant turned and behind him he saw his castle aflame. Tongues of fire stretching up to the sky, the very stone cracking and crumbling in the ungodly heat.

Then, out of the flames strode Gunda, the murdered shepherdess, and Wolfhead, the butchered boarhound. Behind him, the muttering of the bowmen grew angrier, and the giant, feeling his strength sap from his body, backed away as his enemies advanced on him.

Soon he was forced up to the edge of the Penhill cliff, and with a signal from Gunda, the boarhound leapt for the giant's throat. Together they toppled over the cliff, into the mists below, and were never seen again.

In a mighty flash of lightning, and crack of thunder, the men of Penhill were thrown off their feet, and dazed, and when they recovered, the giant's castle had been sundered, and Gunda and the old man had gone.

Pendle Witches

Lancaster, nestled in the northwest of England, and a location that is no stranger to strife over the ages. Once home to a Roman fort, and now the massive Lancaster Castle. The city was raided by the Scots, and is now home to 138,000 people. It is also the location of the infamous Pendleton Witch Trials.

John Law was an itinerant pedlar. A purveyor of household usefuls such as bits of wire, string, mouse-traps, cutlery, cotton, and pins. He was well-known around Lancashire, and he and a little troupe of other pedlars would travel a route around the area visiting villages and towns across the region.

While traveling along the road to Trawdon Forest, he was approached by Alizon Device. It is not clear whether Ms Device was begging, or purchasing, but she wanted some pins, and Mr Law was less than polite, refused to provide pins, and sent her packing with a flea in her ear.

Ms Device was having not a bar of this, and in front of a small crowd of onlookers cursed Mr Law.

It is unfortunate for all concerned with this tale (not least of which the pedlar) that Mr Law shortly thereafter had a stroke, and on his sick-bed blamed this on Alizon Device and her powers of witchcraft.

Alizon Device was subsequently arrested, and brought before the courts. We know this because it is all a matter of official record, in the rather outlandishly titled official documents: The Wonderfull Discoverie of Witches in the Countie of Lancaster, by clerk of the court, Thomas Potts.

Ms Device was questioned, and admitted to Justice Nowell that she had indeed called upon Satan to maim the pedlar.

It is almost certain that this 'questioning' would have been... rigorous... and not what we would consider a reasonable line of questioning in a modern court.

Upon further questioning, Ms Device was a little more forthcoming. She wasn't operating alone, you see... she accused her own grandmother of witchcraft, and another family, in what appears to have been a fairly spiteful act against childhood rivals.

So now we have Alizon Device as the initial witch. Her grandmother (the widow Demdike) and the Chattox family (including the widow Chattox)... all living in proximity to Pendle Hill, in Lancashire.

- It should be noted that these were not particularly well-liked families in the region. They made their livings from healing, begging, theft, and extortion - and were in rivalry with one another. This probably did not endear them to the local communities, and certainly not to the magistrates, who would have known full-well who these people were.

- It should also be pointed out that while England never really had the murderous anti-witch fury of continental Europe... or even the Americas... (Fewer than 500 people were executed for witchcraft in England over a period of around 300 years) witchcraft was considered profoundly evil, and Royally frowned upon. Not only were witches feared in the wider community, but King James I had even written a book (Daemonologie) condemning the practice.

The widow Demdike had been considered a witch for decades. There was actually good money in claiming to have supernatural powers, particularly if you were a purveyor of herbs and medicines, as she was.

The Chattox family and the Demdikes had been rivals for ages, after some altercation involving a burglary and the loss of £1.

Accusations Run Wild

Suddenly, the local villages were up in arms, and deaths which had occurred years previously, of perfectly natural causes (for the era) were now being blamed on this apparent cluster of witches which had now been 'uncovered' in Lancaster.

There was a flurry of infighting among the two accused families, with them hurling accusations at each other, and even within their own ranks, in order to curry favour, avoid blame, and exact revenge.

As this unfurled, several (including Alizon Device) were claiming that they indeed did have magical powers... less concerned perhaps about the risks, and more concerned about preserving their income as practitioners of the supernatural arts.

As a result of the flying accusations, a few more people were dragged into the courts, and detained in the Lancaster Castle dungeons to await a proper trial.

Poorly Timed Rustling

It might have ended there, with some rebuke, censoring, prison time, and what-have-you, if it wasn't for James Device... Alizon's brother, who it seems was something of an idiot, and couldn't leave well enough alone.

One evening, he decided to take the rather poorly timed opportunity to steal a neighbour's livestock, and was caught in the process of cooking a stolen sheep.

A judge decided to open the whole issue back up, and because of this, James Device admitted to a gunpowder plot against parliament (which was nonsense, and likely trumped-up charges by local magistrates looking to make a name for themselves), and a further eight people were questioned for witchcraft, and held in custody for trial.

The Trial Begins in Earnest

The main trial started in August 1612. Perhaps fortunately, the widow Demdike had already died in custody... the dungeon in which everyone was held was cold and damp and horrible.

So... the unfortunate people take the stand - Members of the wider Chattox and Demdike family... Devices, and some other hangers on who were dragged into the debacle by some testimony or other.

Jennet Device

Then in rolls Jennet Device, a nine-year-old girl with a tale to tell.

Under normal circumstances, a nine-year-old would never have been considered a key witness for the prosecution, but thanks to King James and his book Daemonologie, a case was made for suspending the normal rules of evidence for witchcraft trials.

Who knows what pressures had been placed on this poor child, but she provided evidence (and by 'evidence' we mean, she spoke, and it was written down as 'fact') against everyone currently under suspicion for witchcraft... but didn't stop there... she also accused her own mother, and her two siblings.

Of the twelve people who were ultimately accused... eleven were sent to trial, and only one was found not guilty. Nine were found guilty and were immediately executed by hanging.

Alizon Device, Elizabeth Device, James Device, Anne Whittle, Anne Redferne, Alice Nutter, Katherine Hewitt, John Bulcock and Jane Bulcock.

Another, Jennet Preston, was the tenth person found guilty, and sentenced to death by hanging only a few months later.

The Aftermath

Naturally, this whole affair was an absolute travesty, with superstition, property crime, and inter-familial rivalry resulting in the deaths of people who suffered through a legal system in its parochial infancy.

Even Jennet Device, the nine-year old who gave evidence in this trial was herself convicted of witchcraft some 20 or so years later... ironically on the testimony of a ten-year-old boy. She died in prison some time in the late 1630s.

Pendle has a tourism industry around the witches, with local shops profiting from the sale of witch-related bits and pieces. Pendle Hill remains associated with witchcraft, with gatherings held atop it every Halloween.

In the late 1990s a petition was presented to Government asking for the 'witches' to be pardoned (posthumously, obviously) but it was decided that their convictions should stand.

Redcap Powrie

The border between England and Scotland has been a tense one, historically. Let's face it, there's been no love lost between the English and the Scottish for quite some time now... though recent years have seen fewer cavalry charges, and a few more referendums. But conflict attracts... things... that creep around the edges of reality, and the Anglo-Scottish border is where you'd find the Redcap.

Not the old 1960's television series from ITV starring John Thaw... but the vicious little goblin creature from folklore.

The Redcap is a short, chubby member of the fairy-folk with buck-teeth, red eyes, and wrinkled skin. A goblin, or a powrie.

The fingers on each hand are festooned with sharp talons, and long grey hair flows past his shoulders. Sometimes they carry an iron staff, or a bladed weapon.

He wears a stinking red cap, which is made red by dipping it in the blood of his victims.

Basically, think about something that looks a bit like a garden gnome, but with all the charm and personality of a xenomorph from the Alien movies, and you're probably not going to be too far wrong.

The tales vary as to whether there's one particular Redcap, or whether they're a 'type' of goblin... but there are certainly several individual Redcap creatures appearing in folklore.

Some just live in the wilds near the border, and if you happen across them, they will throw stones with unerring accuracy, often killing their victims with a long-range blow to the temple.

Others have allied themselves with morally deficient humans on either side of the border... such as the Redcap which became the familiar of Lord William de Soulis, and caused utter havoc at his orders around Hermitage Castle on the Scottish border.

This ended badly for de Soulis, who according to one legend was wrapped in lead and boiled to death... but that's icky.

These creatures are said to be mostly immune to weaponry, and are far stronger than humans... but they do have a weakness when it comes to scripture - so a few rousing words from your favourite bible will probably see the little blighter off, screaming.

It seems that it's really only the border-Redcap which are vicious and horrible. In other mythology they tend to be more benevolent, such as the Kabouter of Dutch folklore... and the Cornish

Redcaps from south west England are generally described as fairly benevolent.

Near the border, however, they're nasty little creatures - tending to be solo rather than running in groups, and favouring ruined castles for their homes... though they're no strangers to caves and stone circles and the like.

The long and the short of it is that if you see a little fellow wearing a red cap, and you're anywhere other than the Anglo-Scottish border, give him a friendly wave and be about your business.

If you're anywhere between Gretna and Berwick-upon-Tweed, however, you should probably duck and run for cover, because those stones are probably about to start whizzing by.

Redcap Powrie

"...they do have a weakness when it comes to scripture - so a few rousing words from your favourite bible will probably see the little blighter off, screaming."

Storm Kelpies

The mythical na fir ghorma, to use their Gaelic name, are the blue men who ply the waves between the Outer Hebrides and mainland Scotland. They are technically merfolk, who prey on ships with little mercy, and love nothing more than to drag floundering seamen under the waves.

They get the name Storm Kelpies because they tend to attack during storms, and when the weather is calm, they sleep below the waves, out of sight in complex cave systems, and no danger to anyone.

Even when they're awake and on the hunt, if you're a simple fisherman, they were said to simply make their presence known as they swam by - and as long as you gave no offence to them, you would be left to your own devices.

They're also known as "The Blue Men of the Minch", because 'The Minch' is the name of the stretch of water they were said to inhabit.

The term 'kelpie' is usually attributed to some kind of mythical horse, but the na fir ghorma look more or less human apart from their blue colouring.

They were said to swim rather awkwardly, with their upper bodies held out of the waves. A group (school? flock?) of them would likely look rather unusual as they navigated the swell towards their unsuspecting targets.

Similar to other mythical monsters, they don't simply attack. The chief of the na fir ghorma will approach the boat, and call to the captain in rhyme. If the captain answers back with alacrity and wit, they will leave the ship alone. Otherwise it will be dragged into the depths of the ocean.

So, basically, an epic rap battle, with the life of your entire crew on the line. It would therefore seem to make sense for every ship to bring with it a bard, with which to confront these pesky water-Smurfs.

None of the few surviving tales tell of ways to kill the creatures, though it's likely that - while remarkably strong - they're just as vulnerable to iron as any other fae were purported to be - and they were believed to each have regular names (Duncan being one that was written of) with which they identify each other.

Somehow, the concept of being drowned by a mythical blue creature called Gavin, or Barry, is annoying enough that I'd definitely be giving the iron a try. No grasping monster, with a shout of "Get him, Bazil!" is going to drag me beneath the waves!

They are also beneficial, when they're of the mood.

If you were an islander who wanted to fertilise your crops, you would pour ale into the ocean, and that night, the kelpies would leave quantities of rich seaweed on the beach for you to collect.

Their origins are ancient, going back to 500 AD or earlier, and it is posited (among other theories) that they could be descriptions of picts in watercraft like kayaks - their blue-painted skin rising up at right-angles to the water, and giving the terrified sailors the impression that they were swimming with their torsos out of the sea.

Other origin theories suggest that the myths originate with Moorish or North African slaves marooned in Ireland by Vikings.

Tiddy Mun

The East Midlands of England, and the county of Lincolnshire have a long and storied history... but not all of it has been sweetness and light... for in the grimdark of the 16th-19th centuries, the terrible Tiddy Mun stalked the fens.

Now yes, the name is hardly one to inspire fear. I could happily imagine me being on the floor playing with one of the kittens that currently infest our household, and play-fighting with one of them while solemnly intoning "Who's my ickle tiddy mun then?"

It's not a name which invokes spine-tingling terror, like 'Xenomorph' or 'The Thing' or 'Rebooting Fawlty Towers'... but it should.

The Tiddy Mun was a diminutive fellow, no more than three feet tall, with a long white beard, and wearing grey robes so as to blend in with the wilderness. His ilk (for there were more than one of these folk) were also known as the Strangers, Greencoaties and Yarthkins.

Tiddy Mun himself was somewhat aggrieved with people in general.

You see... the Dutch (led by land reclamation expert Cornelius Vermuyden) had drained the fens to open up large swathes of Eastern England for farming. The fens were basically marshland; ecologically diverse areas, and home to all sorts of mythology.

It's at this point that the Tiddy Mun - who apparently lived in the fens - got a bit snippy and started throwing around curses.

These curses tended to involve pestilence. The sort of pestilence that you tended to get when a lot of people suddenly started living and working in what was until recently a swamp. Only a curse could explain that, right?

The only way to lift the curse was to gather all the villagers together at the first twilight of a new moon and poured several buckets of water into the dyke and apologised for the ecological carnage that draining the fens had caused.

I'm not sure I would have been quite so tame about it, but generally - the tale goes - the curse would dissipate, and the Tiddy Mun would glower from the undergrowth, watching for anyone to set a foot out of place.

He wasn't a complete nasty type, however. If there was a flood, in the low-lying regions of Lincolnshire, you could call upon the Tiddy Mun for help.

The cry of "Tiddy Mun wi'out a name, tha watters thruff!" would ring out repeatedly, and the following day the waters would have once-more receded. Because - of course - they wouldn't have if nobody had yelled anything.

Either way, if you kept the Tiddy Mun, and the other Tiddy folk happy, you'd have good harvests, no disease, and generally everything would be fine. If you annoyed them somehow, however - something that was notoriously easy to do quite by accident - then you could find yourself with a jolly good pestilence on your hands.

Thersites the Anti-Hero

Arguably one of the earliest examples of an anti-hero, Thersites was - in mythology - a Greek soldier during the Trojan war. He was described in The Illiad as the ugliest man who came to Troy, who says what everyone else is thinking.

Thersites is certainly portrayed as an ugly and somewhat pathetic figure. He's said to be bow-legged and walk with a pronounced limp. He's got very hunched shoulders, and a pointy head covered in mis-matched tufts of hair.

He first appears in The Illiad (by Homer) briefly, as he interjects while Odysseus and Agamemnon are trying to stir up the Greek troops for an attack.

He has a proper go at Agamemnon, calling him a greedy coward - which is reasonable, given that the general himself was considered rash, impetuous, foolish, irreverent, and inept.

So... Thersites was standing up to say what everyone was apparently thinking - which was rewarded with a thrashing, by Odysseus, which left him crying and the focus of derision.

The Illiad isn't the only place Thersites appears, however...

In Shakespeare's adaptation, Troiluss and Cressida

(1602), Thersites is the slave of the mighty warrior Ajax, and says:

I would thou didst itch from head to foot and I had the scratching of thee; I would make thee the loathsomest scab in Greece

In Goethe's Faust (1832), Thersites appears briefly as a troublemaker, and criticises the events at hand. He is struck by a mace, held by The Lord of Misrule, and this turned him into an egg which hatched into a bat and a snake... but not before whispering:

When some lofty thing is done
I gird at once my harness on.
Up with what's low, what's high eschew,
Call crooked straight, and straight askew

There were a few other appearances as well, but primarily - as with the above - in the form of the social critic... the character who makes a point of criticising the role of the heroes, or the point of the story, as a way to defuse some of the objections, or the more stubborn unwillingness to suspend disbelief.

Thersites is there pointedly to say what everyone is thinking, and while he's ugly and beaten and shamed, because everyone knows you shouldn't just say whatever just pops into your head... and some opinions are... dangerous... he still gets to say it... because when all is said and done, he's just a character in a story, or a play.

Thersites

"I would thou didst itch from head to foot and I had the scratching of thee; I would make thee the loathsomest scab in Greece."

Typhon

If you're not a fan of snakes, you'd likely not be a fan of Typhon. Not only was Typhon (usually, but not always) a snake, but he was a big snake. So powerful was he, that he once sought to overthrow Zeus, and rule the Greek pantheon himself.

Typhon's origins are - naturally - varied, depending on which tale you read first. Technically speaking, Typhon was a monster rather than a God, though most of the tales talk about him being the offspring of one or more Gods - including the Titans who came before the Greek Gods.

The most frequently accepted tale is that Typhon was the son of Gaia and Tartarus, and that eons later he was offended by Zeus in some capacity or other, and decided that he would overthrow the upstart and take everything over for himself.

Some tales describe Typhon as 'pure snake' - others say he was humanoid with snake-like features. It's likely that both are basically true, and that the monster could appear largely how he chose, depending on circumstance. Greek mythology is full of gods and monsters with similar skills, so it's a reasonable supposition.

Either way, when you've got a heavy-hitter like

Zeus fighting a serpentine mega-deity which can stretch across the known-world, you're going to find yourself in something of a brawl... and certainly the fighting was catastrophic.

The only thing that saved Zeus from the massive serpent was his supply of thunderbolts, which he threw with wild abandon, until Typhon was driven back in defeat.

This is the battle that was mentioned earlier in this book, in which the Goddess of War, Enyo, stood back and watched, rather than helping Zeus, in order to maximise the destruction.

You can't kill something like Typhon, of course. Something that had existed before the new Gods, and was one of the first handful of things alive in the universe... the original cosmic horror.

You had to sap its strength and imprison it, and this is what Zeus did, pinning Typhon under the volcanic Mount Etna, in Sicily, where periodically he would coil and uncoil in an attempt to free himself... causing periodic earthquakes and eruptions.

Sir Twardowski

A lot of European folklore deals with the subject of bargains with the devil, and how the - apparently - clever folk making the deals are invariably hoist on their own petard. Poland is no exception, and here is the tale of the Wizard Twardowski.

Depending on which version of the tale you come across, Twardowski didn't start off as a wizard or sorcerer. He was a nobleman in Kraków in the 1500s who was not keen on the idea of mortality, and had a voracious mind for knowledge, especially of the arcane.

He made a deal with the devil stating in which he would be awarded vast knowledge, and magical powers surpassing any other on Earth, making him an incredibly intelligent wizard of unsurpassed might.

Being a bit of a sneaky fellow, Twardowski had a clause inserted into his deal which stated that The Devil could only claim his soul should he ever set foot into Rome - which he had absolutely no intention of doing.

Now, we all know how this sort of thing goes. Either there will be cheating, or there will be some kind of catch, and Twardowski will be off to

Burnytown before you could say "I don't think this is a good idea, mate."

Well... it seemed to be working. For years, Twardowski roamed the land amassing wealth and fame, joining the court of the king (Sigismund Augustus) as his augur. He wrote books about magic, and an encyclopaedia of some renown, summoned ghosts, made a magic mirror... all sorts of things that you'd expect a wizard to do.

He even, at one point, turned a friend into a spider, and kept him as a travelling companion. Which does not seem like a nice thing to do.

One day, however, as Twardowski was sitting in an inn, The Devil appeared to him, grinning, saying it was time to take his soul.

Twardowski was confused. He was still in Poland, and nowhere near Rome. This would seem to have been against the terms of his deal... until The Devil pointed out that the inn was called "Ryzm", which is the Polish word for Rome.

Now, we all know that technically correct is the best form of correct, but Twardowski was having not a jot of it. As he was being slung over The Devil's shoulder for the trip down to the sepulchral depths, he prayed to the Virgin Mary.

According to legend, Mary appeared, giving The Devil quite the fight, and he dropped Twardowski half-way to hell. For some obscure reason, and likely to do with a combination of non-Euclidean geometry, and sheer bloody-mindedness, half-way to hell also happened to be on the moon... so this is where Twardowski lives to this day.

The only company he has is his spider-companion, who he occasionally lets descend to Earth on a silken thread to bring him news from the realms he once knew.

There is some supposition that the tale was based on a real historical character; either a German nobleman who was born in Nuremberg and later moved to Kraków - or one of two scientists (John Dee or Edward Kelley) - both of whom were believed to have lived in Kraków at the time of the tale.

Will o' the Wisp

A rare but natural phenomenon, the wisp-like lights sometimes seen in marshlands is thought to be produced by bioluminescence, or chemiluminescence brought about by the oxidation of chemicals produced through organic decay. But the folklore around them is quite startling.

Britain

The tales in Britain tell of miscreants doomed to forever haunt the night-time marshes for some villainy or other. In one notable story, a wicked blacksmith is rebuffed at the gates of Heaven but given one last chance to live a good life on Earth. Failing to do so, he is given a single piece of burning coal to warm his tattered soul and is cast into the marshes. He will occasionally use the burning ember to lure unwitting mortals into the marshes, to their doom.

In Wales, the lights are tiny goblin-like pwca who lead travellers off the beaten path into the bogs, and then extinguish their lights, mischievously leaving them lost.

Ireland

An Irish version of the tale has a notorious trickster who, upon having his soul claimed by The Devil, manages to trap the devil not once, but twice, therefore prolonging his life for decades. When he eventually does die, his wickedness means he cannot enter Heaven, and the Devil refuses him entry as an act of revenge... forcing him to walk the dark, wet places of the Earth for eternity - with (again) only a single ember to light his way.

The Americas

In the Americas, the wisps are said to be returned souls which attack the living for vengeance, or the offspring of a vampiric witch that take the form of a flame at night.

Asia

In some parts of Asia, the lights are seen as ghosts of drowned sailors, who help the living avoid dangers. In other areas, they are phantom children of mythical Yokai demons.

So...

They're not always bad, but in most of the tales around the world where wisps can be sighted, they are generally considered to be portentous at best, and villainous at worst.

Certainly actually seeing the effect at night can be remarkably eerie, and whether it is bioluminescence, chemiluminescence, plant-life or insects; it's bound to be un-nerving if you're alone in the dark... and it is no wonder that such creepy tales have grown up around them.

Whaitiri

Whaitiri is a female goddess in Māori mythology, and her role is as the personification of thunder. Alas, she is also a cannibal, and feels somewhat lonely in the skies.

According to the legends, she hears tales of a mortal man who dwells on Earth, called Kaitangata. In Māori, Kai is the word for food, and tangata is the word for people... so Kaitangata translates loosely as man-eater.

As Whaitiri is fond of her cannibalism, she feels that Kaitangata would make a fantastic husband, so she summons her power, and during a great storm, descends to Earth and marries him.

How this marriage occurs is not really gone into in any of the texts I've read. I will admit to not being an expert on Māori mythology, but it seems like quite a lot of the backstory might have been skipped at this point. Just "Ooh, he looks nice" followed by THUNDER and suddenly, "you're married, mate."

As a gift to her new husband, Whaitiri kills a slave, and offers the heart and liver to him. The problem is that Kaitangata is cursed with a rather misleading name. He's not a cannibal at all, but a hard-working, kindly man, and he's horrified by what his new wife has just done.

He implores her to not eat people anymore, and - as a fisherman - says that he will instead catch fish for her. Watching him fish, Whaitiri realises that he has never learned to make a barbed fishhook, so she offers him this knowledge as a gift instead of the slave's innards... and he is pleased.

With a new barbed hook, he catches a large fish, which Whaitiri offers to the gods.

So, for a while everything is well. Kaitangata is doing much better as a fisherman, because he now has barbed hooks... and Whaitiri is not eating people... but she soon grows tired of a diet of fish.

One day, when her husband is away fishing, Whaitiri takes up a net, and captures and kills two of her husband's relatives, who were hunting in the forest nearby.

She does not know the proper rituals to cleanse the bodies, but even so, she cuts them up and gorges herself on their flesh, until only the bones are left. Unbeknown to her, she has been seen by the villagers, and word soon gets back to Kaitangata, who decides that enough is enough.

Kaitangata uses the bones of his relatives to make fishhooks, and catches fish to give to Whaitiri. She eats the fish - which is infused with the tapu[10] of the bones (because the proper rituals were not performed) of the two slaughtered men... and this causes Whaitiri to go blind, so that she can no longer hunt humans.

One day, not too long afterwards, she is making her way slowly through the village when she overhears her husband describe her as having a heart as cold as snow, and that she is basically not a good wife because she does not look after their children.

Ashamed and angry, she confesses to Kaitangata that she is the embodiment of thunder, and she gathers the last of her power, and leaves the village wrapped in a cloud, leaving him and her two sons on Earth.

And this is the last we hear of Whaitiri for a while, until many decades later, when her grandchildren, having heard the tales of their grandmother from the skies, tried to climb up into the heavens.

At the foot of the climb, they find Whaitiri, who has not been able to ascend due to her blindness... and instead, she has been grubbing around in the dirt growing tubers and taro.

Ysbaddaden Pencawr

The tale of Ysbaddaden is linked to the Arthurian legends (and Welsh folklore) that many people might be familiar with, but as a sort-of off-shoot of the main tale which is usually not covered in the classics.

Ysbaddaden is a chief of giants. He is destined to die when his daughter, the beautiful Olwen, marries. As you can imagine, he's therefore less than keen for her to marry. He has been a bit of a scourge of the surrounding area. He's tormented and killed his way throughout Wales and caused any amount of mayhem. He's not very popular, but he's pretty tough.

Specifically: In the medieval Welsh tale *Culhwch ac Olwen* that we're talking about here, he is the cruel and vicious king of the giants, who defeated the former ruler and killed his 23 children.

Culhwch - the 'hero' of our tale - is the son of King Cilydd son of Celyddon. When the King's wife dies, and he re-marries, the somewhat evil stepmother tries to get him to marry his stepsister.

At this point, unless you're Welsh, the pronunciation of these names is probably causing you some consternation. I'd recommend just letting it flow over you, and look it up later when you've calmed down. Welsh is a pretty interesting language, but not much sounds like it looks written down.

This sort of carry-on might be a popular search on Pornhub, but Culhwch wasn't having a bar of it, and rebuffed his stepmother's 'suggestion'. As a result, she reveals her true nature and in a fit of pique curses Culhwch to only have eyes for Olwen, daughter of Ysbaddaden.

Culhwch is therefore smitten with Olwen, even though he's never met her. He goes to his cousin Arthur (*the* Arthur) for help. Arthur provides him with some knights and some weapons, and a bit of advice, so Culhwch nips off to find the elusive Olwen.

The meaning of the name Olwen is "white footprint". According to legend, she was so gentle and fragile that white trefoils would grow in her footprints.

Olwen ultimately treats him favourably and decides she would like to marry him. Which is nice, isn't it? Certainly, the whole tale would have been a bit dead-ended if she'd just crossed her arms, sniffed imperiously, and said "Ew! No thanks. My mother told me never to trust a ginger."

Unfortunately, she can't marry him unless Ysbaddaden agrees, and since the giant's life is tied to her unmarried status, he's not keen... but it's a bit political, so rather than have the whole thing turn into a scuffle - as it would have - Ysbaddaden tells Culhwch that he will agree to the marriage...

IF (That's right, there's always an 'if'...)

IF Culhwch completes a series of forty tasks, each more fiendish and devious than the last.

As an aside: Actually, before announcing the tasks, there was an unfortunate incident with a poison dart, but it came to nothing, so it really was in Ysbaddaden's best interests - given the presence of Arthur's knights at this point - to try to contain the situation, and hope that Culhwch's over-eagerness would be his undoing.

As the tale is fragmentary, it's not known what all of the tasks were, but to give you a bit of a taste of the sort of thing... two of them were:

- Obtain the basket/hamper of Gwyddneu Garanhir (The elfin ruler of a sunken land off the coast of Wales)
- Hunt Ysgithyrwyn, the chief boar.

It goes without saying that Culhwch completes the tasks - though the fragmentary nature of the tale doesn't give all the details.

Presumably he approached Gwyddneu Garanhir and said, "I'll give you a tenner for the basket", and approached Ysgithyrwyn and said "Eat spiky spear-laden death, giant pig-monster!".

With the help of Arthur's knights, Culhwch returns, victorious to Olwen, and things go a bit bad for Ysbaddaden.

Because he's annoyed so many people, and because Arthur's knights are still floating about, the people who have been affronted by the giant all turn up to take their revenge. The giant is ritually humiliated, flayed alive, and beheaded by his own nephew.

Culhwch and Olwen happily marry at this point. She and her father were not close, I guess. Still, I can't help but think that having a wedding while there was a giant's head on a spike in the dining-room would have put a bit of a damper on the evening - even if he was a villain.

The tale bears a few similarities to Tolkien's Tale of Beren and Lúthien, though the Bride-Quest theme is strong in quite a lot of Western folklore. Either way, a fairly niche but quite interesting mythological villain.

Yacumama of the Peruvian Deltas

Many cultures and regions have myths and legends about giant serpents. Snakes and serpents in general were often dangerous, so it's natural that a bigger one would be seen as pretty scary by the local producers of myth and legend.

It is no different in the wilds of Peru which, apart from being home to marmalade-loving bears named after English train stations, there are many tales of gods and monsters. Not the least of which is Yacumama, the giant serpent.

The tale of Yacumama is believed to go all the way back to the Incan civilisation of around the 13th century... and possibly further back than that.

This creature is described as - well, as we've said - a giant serpent. It is well-known among the Quechua people of the Peruvian rainforest, though is certainly not exclusive to them... being described widely among many indigenous groups as quite similar to an anaconda, only gigantic in scale.

Now, given that an anaconda can already reach 22 feet or so (the largest yet discovered being 27-33ft in length, depending on which source you prefer) then someone saying "Like an anaconda, only gigantic" is not a description I'm comfortable with at the best of times.

Some variations of the tale suggest that Yacumama is around 200ft long... which is the same length as around 14.3 giraffes, or 1/36168th the length of Wales, which ever measurement system you prefer.

So, apart from being quite big what's the deal with this snake?

Yacumama is said to be the mother of all sea creatures... though I'm not sure whether this means that it is the actual physical mother of each and every sea creature... which seems unlikely... or whether she's the original source from which all sea creatures ultimately sprung - in some kind of serpentine origin story.

She is also said to be able to slurp up prey from over 100 paces away, regardless of the size or strength of the creature.

In order to protect themselves from Yacumama, indigenous people are said to have blown on a conch horn before getting into water deeper than their knees... as Yacumama was curious, and would pop her head up above the water.

Clearly, the idea being, if a 200ft snake popped its head up above the water and looked at you... you don't go in there if you know what's good for you.

Yaushikep and Akkorokamui

According to folklore, atop a great mountain in Hokkaido, Japan, in ancient times there was a giant red spider called Yaushikep. If you're not a big fan of spiders, then you might not mind this particular one too much, because there was an unusual comeuppance.

This spider wasn't just big in the sense that you'd freak out if you saw it. It was far greater than Shelob in terms of size... if you remember your Lord of the Rings. It was big in the sense that it towered over buildings, and spanned a hectare in size. (10,000m^2), so quite the eight-legged behemoth.

As a result, Yaushikep was particularly dangerous, and it took to terrorising a village at the base of the mountain. It's not clear whether it did so on purpose, but the beast's footsteps shook the village, destroyed houses, and had the poor villagers running for the nearby hills.

Every time Yaushikep passed by - which was frequently - houses would fall, rocks would tumble, and people would be terrified, injured, and killed.

Eventually, they had enough, and as a group they appealed to the gods for help.

The only god who answered their cries was Repun

Kamuy, the Ainu god of the sea, and he waited until Yaushikep once more descended from the mountain, and as the houses began to shake, he dragged it down the mountain, and submerged it in the waters of Uchiura Bay, in Hokkaido.

You'd think this would be the end of it. A sea god drowning a giant spider... but no. Repun Kamuy had no intention of killing the creature. He had been trying to find a creature to protect the waters around the bay.

Instead of being drowned, Yaushikep was transformed into an equally gigantic octopus, and assumed the new title of Akkorokamui.

No longer inherently villainous, Akkorokamui was nevertheless fickle and dangerous. If the best took offence to your passing by in your fishing vessel, it would still try to sink it... and fishermen were said to carry scythes on their vessels in-case of an attack.

For the most part, however, Akkorokamui, if you could avoid the monster's ire, was rather more benevolent than when it was the spider Yaushikep. It was now endowed with powers to heal and bestow knowledge to those who were most deserving and, presumably, asked nicely.

Mostly, however, those travelling on the water were safe unless the waters turned red, for this meant that Akkorokamui was rising, and was likely displeased about something. For this reason, a red tide would mean that the fishermen would stay home, rather than risk the wrath of the giant octopus.

Yaushikep

"Every time Yaushikep passed by - which was frequently - houses would fall, rocks would tumble, and people would be terrified, injured, and killed."

AFTERTHOUGHT

The Nursery Rhyme

I'm not sure these are even a thing anymore, but when I was a kid, we learned a lot of nursery rhymes. I imagine that in today's high-tech world, a lot of those are going to be forgotten...

People have this tendency to ascribe meaning to them which does not seem to be backed up by a great deal - as if the wisdom of the ages was being passed down from child to child in some form of cryptographic short-hand... which is almost certainly mostly nonsense.

Oh, some have a particular learning theme... *Thirty-days-hath-September* springs immediately to mind as a mnemonic for remembering how many days each month has.

Heck, I still recite that one in my head periodically. Once we get around the whole June/July/August end of the year, I'm far too exhausted to remember how many days they're all supposed to have. Mnemonics are handy like that.

Humpty-Dumpty is said to be about a cannon, even though all the pictures seem to show 'him' being an egg... so who knows, right?

The egg thing is actually fairly recent. I assume because eggs are particularly breaky. However, if you were an egg-man of some description, I would imagine you'd go out of your way to avoid walls.

One of the oldest known surviving nursery rhymes is "Pat-a-cake, pat-a-cake, baker's man", with references going all the way back to the mid-16th century but there are plenty which we think are quite old, but are in fact relatively contemporary.

Let's start with some of the classics:

BAA BAA BLACK SHEEP
Much pilloried of late for apparently being racist... some schools locally even opted to change the sheep to green, though I never really understood why the colour of a sheep would have any racist connotations. There were some unfounded suppositions in the UK in the 1980s that the rhyme was about the slave trade.

"Hey kids! Here's a fun rhyme about the abomination of slavery and indentured servitude! Everyone got your skipping ropes! Yaaay!" - Said nobody, ever. Outside of Virginia, North/South Carolina, and Maryland, anyway.

The rhyme is used as something of a political stabbing point about political correctness run mad, but most comments to this effect are based on a relatively small number of incidents where a particular school or two have - as above - made changes to the lyrics, but not because of some wider spread government policy.

In truth, it is considered far more likely that the rhyme was about an unpopular policy of wool taxation in England in the late 1700s... which is the period in which this nursery rhyme was first recorded. There's a reasonable amount of documentation which supports this... but let's be fair... at face value, which is all the kids are going to understand anyway... it's about a sheep.

As an interesting aside, this rhyme was the first recorded song to be played by a computer, all the way back in 1951.

The rhyme itself is sung to the same tune as Twinkle Twinkle Little Star...

I know a couple of you have just sat bolt upright and gone "OMFG!" over that.

... and has a few variations. The modern one tends to follow this format:

Baa, baa, black sheep, Have you any wool?
Yes, sir, yes, sir, Three bags full;
One for the master, One for the dame,
And one for the little boy Who lives down the lane.

RING-A-RING-O-ROSIE

While you'd think this one has been around for a heck of a long time, it's actually relatively recent compared to a lot of traditional nursery rhymes. It is first recorded in the 1840s, as part of a children's game where everyone joins hands and dances around in a circle, only to fall down at the last line.

Having said that, a very similar German variant was recorded in the late 1790s, and it is quite likely that the English version is based on this.

It's true. England stole a lot of German tales, folklore, traditions, and nursery rhymes. Later, the United States did much the same thing with their rocketry programs.

The general understanding is that the rhyme is about the Plague, which ravaged Europe... but in truth, it is rather more contemporary than that, and the 'symptoms' recorded in the rhyme bear no similarity to this particular disease.

Other diseases rocked Europe of course, so it could comfortably have been one of those... but the references to the plague don't even appear in conjunction with this rhyme until the middle of the 20th century.

The rhyme has also been linked to Pagan mythology and practices, again without too much evidence.

In truth, if it genuinely was adapted from the German rhyme, then it's probably just some pretty verse which has been mutated along the way.

Ring-a-ring o' roses, A pocket full of posies,
A-tishoo! A-tishoo! We all fall down.

Ringel, Ringel, Rosen, (A ring, a ring o' roses)
Schöne Aprikosen, (Lovely apricots)
Veilchen blau, Vergissmeinnicht, (Violets blue, forget-me-nots)
Alle Kinder setzen sich! (Sit down, children all!)

GEORGIE PORGIE

First documented in the 1840s, this one was described as a 'traditional ballad'. Traditional or not, this nursery rhyme seemed to be used more as a taunt for fat kids (or kids called George) than anything in recent decades.

Oddly, the name George remains very popular. It has been in the top 200 European names for quite a long time according to US Social Security Administration data... though honestly, if you asked me to write down 200 names, chances are I'd run into trouble after a few dozen.

There isn't really a great deal of history or story behind this one, and while the 1840s documentation suggests it's a traditional old ballad, chances are it wasn't all that old. It's certainly not mentioned in anything much older than that.

Some references suggest that it was something of a rebuke against King George I, who was apparently not well-liked... but again, this hasn't come from the source, and is based on much-copied supposition.

Georgie Porgie, pudding and pie, Kissed the girls and made them cry, When the girls came out to play, Georgie Porgie ran away.

Of note, the version I learned, the third line was boys, not girls.

SO WHAT?

Realistically, they're just fun rhyming nonsense phrases to jump about to when you're a child.

Like a lot of the early years stuff, which is passed along over the ages, what really are the chances that some adult sat down and encoded some deeply philosophical point about disease, or danger, into a song, and then told the kids to go and skip to it?

They're fascinating because they're probably about the last surviving oral tradition in the West. Kids pick these things up more from each other, and it's only been in recent years that people have been paying too much attention to them and 'teaching' new versions with sanitised or modernised lyrics.

I say we just leave them alone. Little soap-bubbles of history floating up through the years, in some way insulating ever-so-slightly against the technology, and advertising, and cynical corporate grabs at kiddie's heartstrings to empty their parent's pockets.

Moon and Lunacy

The moon is a bit of a fall-guy for our failings, our villainy, and our lunacy. Even the very word 'lunacy' has its root in 'lunar'.

Werewolves love it. Regular wolves howl at it. Crime goes up when its full. Vampires probably get mild sunburn from it. It is, if you believe some myths and legends, the source of many an evil.

A lot of this is nonsense, of course. Crime doesn't go up during a full moon... there have been actual scientific studies... but the moon genuinely does influence a lot on Earth... from tides to mass animal migration... so where the heck did all this mythology come from?

The Moon is an astronomical body orbiting Earth and is the planet's only natural satellite. It is the fifth-largest satellite in the Solar System, and by far the largest among planetary satellites relative to the size of the planet that it orbits. It has a radius of 1,737 km, and a surface gravity of 1.62m/s(sq).
- Wikipedia

This physical description doesn't answer some of the metaphysical questions... some of which are surprisingly recent.

Did you know, for example, that if you committed a crime in the 1800s in England, you could petition for a lighter sentence if you happened to commit that crime under a full moon? That's right... "The Moon made me do it" was genuinely a mitigating factor in your sentence!

At the Bedlam lunatic asylum (which was admittedly a horrifying place) certain psychiatric maladies were treated by chaining up and flogging someone during a full moon.

When you look back in history, the Moon has been embodied with malice for thousands of years. Hippocrates once wrote:

One who is seized with terror, fright and madness during the night is being visited by the goddess of the moon

It's reasonable for so much of our historical focus to be taken up by the Moon. I mean, for most of human history it was the single most striking object in the sky at night. In a world without streetlights, what else would there be to do but sit in your tree, trying not to be eaten by sabre-toothed cats, and gazing at the Moon?

The moon was often the opposite of the life-giving sun. The 'nice' gods of the daylight gave way to the 'nasty' gods of the night. The white wolf that chases the golden deer. The goddess who rides her silver chariot across the skies at night, forever in pursuit of the day.

Why she couldn't just stop and wait for him is another story, I guess. Gods always seem to be a bit dim about such things.

Ovid tells the tale of old King Lycaon, who served the gods a meal of human flesh, and was turned into the first werewolf as punishment.

Ew.

In modern times, the Moon has been the home of Icke's lizard race, who secretly rule the world (there's some old school villainy for you), and of course there are the moon-landing deniers, and the new 'race' to land there and see whether or not permanent colonies are an option.

There are exciting things coming for the Moon, and not all of them are likely to be villainous... but it's interesting just how much weirdness has linked to it over the course of human history.

The Debunked Myth

We all love a good yarn. Some little tale of wisdom that makes us snerkle into our cornflakes (other breakfast cereals are available) and think about how we wouldn't have fallen for whatever logical trap some supposedly smart folk did. Like the pens at NASA.

As the tale goes, NASA was happily sending astronauts into space at the start of the space race, and discovered quite early on that the ballpoint pens with which they had been equipping them simply didn't work in zero gravity.

You see, the ink needs gravity to flow down the pen. Get a standard ballpoint pen and try to write upside down with it... you'll soon see that the ink runs out and it just stops working.

This is terrible, because apparently in space in the 1960s, you needed to write a lot down using ballpoint pens. Presumably angst-ridden poems about the curvature of the Earth, and how pretty the aurora looks out of the window of your tin can... that sort of thing.

Anyway... it was a problem just begging for a solution, so NASA spent ten years and hundreds of millions of dollars to develop a pressurised pen that would work in zero gravity, and write on almost any surface. In typical over-engineering form, they supposedly made it so that it could write at temperatures ranging from below freezing to almost the boiling point of water.

The development of this pen meant that NASA astronauts could now write things down in space, without having to constantly do that thing where you flick the pen or wave it around at the end of your arm - like so many of us have done to get the last little dregs of ink to settle on the ball so we can finish off our diary entries without having to go find another one.

Dear diary. Today watched the cat snooze in a sunbeam and decided that I would much rather be a cat than a person. Apparently some people are in space. Isn't that nice?

The Russian cosmonauts, on the other hand - in some presumably very smug manner - simply used a pencil.

Дорогой дневник. Трактор сломан. У меня хромота. Моего дядю съели волки. По крайней мере, у меня есть этот карандаш.

The story is of course one of over-engineering the solution to a very minor problem, of unconscionable waste, and of supposedly wise people being remarkably stupid and short-sighted.

The story is of course, complete and utter arse-caramel.

Simply put, during the dawn of spaceflight, everybody used a pencil. The Russians, the Americans, and... well, that was about it, really.

The point is that in the vasty deeps of the yawning *Cthulhian Beyond*, where the elder gods fitfully slumber as the universe flickers around them like some kind of vaporous flame... nobody was using a ballpoint pen.

Pencils come with their own special problems, however. The 'lead' isn't lead at all, but graphite, and graphite is a rather good conductor of electricity. Using a pencil creates tiny dusty fragments of graphite, which can float through the pure oxygen inside the space podule... because in the early days of space travel, pure oxygen was how they did it. None of this nitrogen nonsense.

All it would take would be for one, tiny, crossed circuit, one tiny flicker of an electric arc, and your oxygen-filled podule would simply combust, killing everyone on board.[11]

So, the issue was that a suitable replacement needed to be found, and this came in the form of the ballpoint pen. Not just a standard ballpoint pen, because it is true that it wouldn't work in zero gravity for all the reasons named above... but NASA didn't spend hundreds of millions of dollars.

They did start to develop a pen to meet their requirements, but they cancelled the program when costs threatened to blow out. The mantle was taken up by private industry, particularly Austrian *Friedrich Schächter* and the Fisher Space Pen company, who spent around a million dollars on initial development.

Not just to design the pen, but to put some machinery into place to start manufacturing it on a small scale.

Subsequently, in 1967 it is generally taken as gospel that NASA tested the design, and then decided to purchase approximately 400 pens at US$6 each (roughly US$45 in today's money) for use in any subsequent Apollo missions.

Admittedly, this was a lot for a pen at the time... but we are talking about the multi-billion-dollar space industry here, and they could likely handle the cost. The Russians bought them too... because they were just as committed to avoiding fires on their spacecraft.

Дорогой дневник. У нас есть значительные идеологические разногласия с Западом, но из них получается хорошее перо.

And yet the same trite old myth is rolled out every

year, in spite of all of the evidence to the contrary, that NASA spent hundreds of millions creating a pen, while the Russians just used a pencil.

AFTERWORD

And there we have it. I hope you enjoyed the read as much as I enjoyed writing it. I certainly learned about a few unusual critters of the folklore variety while I was doing the research, and I hope a few of them at least were new to you too.

If you've made it this far, and come to the end of the book, then I applaud your perseverance. Imagine a loud *"DING!"* and bright floaty letters proudly proclaiming "Achievement Unlocked". You are now well prepared for the test.

If you've just jumped straight to this bit... that's a bit weird.

But I guess if you're still reading then you'll want to know a little bit about me. I'm fairly resigned to the fact that I'm unlikely to retire on the proceeds of my writing... but I enjoy the process, so I guess I'll keep going.

I live in New Zealand, which is a pretty little country quite frequently left off maps, to the right-hand side of Australia. I have a wife, a small child, and two kittens. More or less in that order, depending on who is demanding most of my attention at the time. I wasn't born in New Zealand... I'm Welsh. Having arrived here before turning two years old, I can reliably inform you that I've lost most of my Welsh accent.

If you're after heroic tales of derring-do, you're mostly out of luck. My idea of a hair-raising adventure these days is trying to figure out how to change a lawnmower blade or hang a door.

I also run a Facebook group called *Villainy* (with four other very helpful volunteers) where most of the content for the books gets its first experimental airing before being compiled into book form. I can refine it there, you see, and test it across multiple groups before deciding whether I should give it a tweak or two:

http://www.facebook.com/groups/TopVillains

Thank you for buying my book. Whether it's on Kindle, or made of actual dead trees, I appreciate it, and define my self-worth by how much you enjoy it. Feel free to drop me a note at:

villainybooks@mordorbbs.com

Rob Mordor
New Zealand
November 2022

FOOTNOTES

---

[1] Moorlands in southern England, around Devon.

[2] It seems that Pliny's world was full of horrors and wonders which we certainly don't put much credence in now... but imagine living in the belief that such things roamed the world.

[3] "Totes Amazeballs" from the Latin. Tot, meaning "many", and Ama, meaning "water bucket", and... Zeballs probably being an ancient King who had too many buckets. Or something.

[4] I mean, it sounds rather pretty... but if you're just going to bang on it with a stick or something, I don't really see the point.

[5] Available for free download, if you are lucky enough to find it in English.

[6] Neither did my Pohutukawa. Something I am, to this day, quite bitter about.

[7] Low-lying boggy marshland.

[8] Traditional folk song. Author unknown.

[9] Not to be confused with Great Uncle Bulgaria, who is

in Wimbledon.

[10] A sacredness, or spiritual restriction.

[11] This actually happened in Apollo 1, 1967, where an electrical fault caused the oxygen to ignite and killed a number of US astronauts, including Virgil "Gus" Grissom, Edward H. White II, and Roger B. Chaffee.

Printed in Great Britain
by Amazon